Confessions of a Stripper

By

Terra Angelique

names, characters, places, and incidents are entirely coincidental.

For information, contact silverdynastypublications@yahoo.com

Chapter 1
Kayla

Today I would dance harder than I ever had before. Most people wouldn't consider this a career because they're too simple-minded; too focused on the moral point of view. They believed that every stripper was just a low down dirty hoe that was out there trying to make a quick buck instead of actually working a 9 to 5 job.

My thing is, none of these motherfuckers had ever tried to look at the whole "unholy ass career" in a point of view that wouldn't make motherfucker's like me feel so filthy.

Yes, I was in it for the money, but the money wasn't the root. My main reason was to start a new life; a life where success was guaranteed, and failure was nonexistent. See I was from Dallas, the Triple D., where bad bitches came a dime a dozen. Everybody knows that everything's always bigger in Texas.

"I have to show these motherfuckers what I'm made of." I said out loud as I looked at myself in the full body mirror in the locker room.

My ass was luscious if I must say so myself. I could sit two cups on it and shake what my momma gave me without the cup tipping over. I must have been thinking a little too hard because next thing I know a dancer named, Trixie, slapped my ass and said, "Damn bitch I know you hear them calling ya name!"

I just looked at her and said, "My bad I was lost in thought."

"Well bitch you ain't got no time to be thinking in here. It's time to run them bands up." She said bending over making her knees touch her elbows while shaking her ass out of control.

All I could do was laugh as she came back up doing the stripper walk.

"Girl you crazy as hell, I'm not bout to play with you!"

I walked towards the door leading to the stage waiting for the infamous DJ, *DJ Town*, to announce my name, once again. I couldn't help but think about Trixie's monkey see, monkey do looking ass while I waited. If Trixie loved money more than she loved being a hoe she would be the one closing the show. Trixie always found a way to make extra cash and it wasn't by shaking her ass; it was by selling it. That was just something I wasn't with.

One night, after the show, I left my phone on the desk where we did our makeup. I grabbed it and was about to walk out until I heard loud ass moans coming from the area where the floor strippers gave private lap dances. The club had been closed at least 2 hours, so I didn't know why anybody would be back there.

So, like a typical white girl in a scary movie, I slowly went to check it out. I opened the curtain just enough for one eye to peek through and saw Trixie, positioned just like a monkey. She was in a handstand giving head to an upcoming artist by the name of Kodak. My knee bumped into the table and I had to cover my mouth to avoid making a sound, but they still heard me because a nigga jerked back.

"BITCH! I thought you said nobody was here, I'm out! Can't fuck with you grimey hoes." He snapped.

Kodak pulled up his pants and started back bumping his gums. "Yeah, you can strip, but ya head game weak as fuck. Learn how to use that mouth without scraping a nigga dick with ya teeth." And just like that, he was out.

I went further inside and sat down by Trixie.

"So, what the fuck were you trying to do? Bitch the club been closed!" I asked her.

"I was just trying to make a quick come up. The nigga was talking about 5 thousand just to suck him up," Trixie said.

I watched her fight back the tears that were welling up in her eyes. I kept looking around out trying to decide whether I should leave this dumb hoe. Looking up at the ceiling I sighed. I decided to go against my better judgment. I helped her ass up and told her, "That stupid ass shit ain't the way to come up hoe. See that's exactly why strippers get frowned upon now because of dumb bitches like you always on some other shit."

Trying to calm down and be cool, I just closed my mouth with no apologies intended for her ass. She had to be embarrassed. So, I just kept my mouth shut, not allowing anything else to come out that could make her feel more than the whore she was.

I made sure she made it to her car and told her to call me when she got home. Unfortunately, the call never came. In the weeks to follow, Trixie was going around saying she got raped by the artist. Well, at least that's what I'd heard. But I didn't believe everything that I hear. The next time I saw Trixie was 3 months later. She had made a come up for herself by selling the story to TMZ for half a million dollars.

They ate that shit up. I never got a chance to confront her about it, but God don't like ugly. Her ass ended up back where she started. In the club shaking her ass for a buck because the IRS took every last dime she had. My thoughts were interrupted when I heard DJ Town announce me.

"And now to the stage. The sexy black stallion Crystal with a C. Now let me hear them hands clap."

Whenever I was on stage, I'd be in a zone. I was covered in glitter from head to toe with my Red Bottoms on and a bad ass red Monokini. You couldn't help but notice every aspect of my figure. Everything popped out in all the right places. My song of choice to dance to was "Pony remix" by Chris Brown. I placed my right hand on the pole and wrapped my right leg around it. In one swift motion I was upside down with my legs spread out in the shape of a V making both cheeks clap together to every beat. I slid back down and flipped upright and came down in a split while bouncing up and down.

After that I came back up in a backward handstand against the pole. Pulling myself up, I let my legs spread out like an eagle and swung around the pole. Then I pulled my legs towards the pole and rode the pole all the way down like I was on a motorcycle. When I planted my Red Bottoms back on the platform, I bent all the way down and let my ass shake. There was nothing but hundreds, fifties, twenties, and ones scattered everywhere. I kicked one leg up and held the heel of my shoe and spun all the way around in a complete circle and dropped in another split one last time as the song ended. Out the corner of my eye I saw Trixie's ass back where I left her looking crazy just like a hating ass bitch.

As I exited the stage I made sure to pick up every piece of money lying around me. I was trying to catch my breath as well. I could hear DJ

Town and the niggas going crazy. In the midst of everything Trixie ass had the nerve to grab my arm and say

"Bitch that was good and all, but you need to tone it up. Looking all tired and shit, one of these days you gone hurt yaself!"

I looked at her like 'bitch bye' and then told her ass with the quickness, "Baby, everything I do is on a whole other level than you!" Then I walked off.

I didn't have time for washed up ass hating hoes. I walked back into the locker room with the other girls and stuffed my money in my gym bag and was about to freshen up when suddenly I felt a hard slap on my ass making my ass cheek sting a little which pissed me off.

My reflexes instantly kicked in causing me to jerk my head and body around so fast that you would think I was trying to snatch a motherfucker soul. I took a deep breath and tried to focus on who in the hell was back here invading my space because the area was restricted for anyone who wasn't a dancer.

I slid my hand over my face regrouping myself, then looked ahead to see Kodak grinning like he just knew he was the shit. The way he was looking at me was like he wasn't gone let go until he undressed me. Shit I knew I looked good, but damn, he was acting like he had lost his fucking mind. I must've been looking at his ass long and hard because he looked me up and down and said, "You can chill with all that, fix ya face ma. You cute lil' momma but you ain't that cute and you was never bad, so listen to a nigga like me."

Rolling my eyes, I turned back around and started grabbing my shit. My blood was fucking boiling! I don't know who the fuck he thought he was but I damn sure wasn't anything like Trixie. I don't suck dick for money, I bounce my ass for an audience for mine.

He must have been confused. I started picking up my make-up that was remaining on my desk area as he leaned his back against it, putting his hands on my shoulder like he knew me. I shot him a quick glance like 'nigga what is you doing'. He licked his lips and began again talking again.

"Chill ma. I didn't come here for no mess I just wanted to let you know I liked what I saw. Shit apparently all the other niggas did too ya dig. I be on the road going city to city, and I ain't ever, I mean ever, saw a bitch do some tricks like that! I want you to dance for me and I don't mean in private. I mean in groups. Like for me and my niggas. I'm gone let you know off hand the pay would be way more than you make here in a night."

I was already starting to get annoyed. I started changing back into my regular clothes, a pair of American eagle boot cut jeans and a tank top and was throwing my Nikes on. Before he could even get finished speaking, I stopped him.

"I'm good, I'm not looking for no new business ventures right now homie."

That nigga looked at me with ice cold eyes and said, "Homie? Say check this out. I ain't no bum ass nigga out here off the streets shawty. I was trying to help ya ass out".

He started reaching for my ass as I bent down to close my gym bag. I shifted to the right. "I'm good."

As I was about to walk off I saw Trixie standing at the door like she was watching the whole time. She turned around and went back out the door. By the time I made it outside the club she was nowhere to be found. I took my keys out and hit the unlock button to my Chrysler 300. That bitch was my baby. She was sitting right with the 22 inch rims and burnt red paint, my favorite color. After sitting my gym bag in the back seat, I hopped in the front and made my way to my one bedroom townhouse.

My house was only a 20 minute drive from the club, but I was the cautious type of motherfucker that never let a bitch or a nigga know where I stay. Besides, there's only one real bitch on my team, and that's Tesea aka Diamond. We had been friends since the 10th grade and she ain't ever let me down. She knew everything about me and knew exactly what buttons to push and what buttons not to.

While in deep thought I pulled in my driveway and hopped out the car and opened up the back driver's side door. Scanning the whole backseat, I grabbed my gym bag and pulled it over my shoulder. I couldn't lie I was tired as fuck, I didn't know why but all of a sudden, I started swaying back and forth and my vision became blurry.

I grabbed onto the door handle of my car trying to keep my balance, but I was barely able to grip it because my hands were sweating so damn bad. Nothing at that moment made any damn sense whatsoever. I looked all around, up and down the street trying to take deep breaths while at the same time trying to see if anyone was around; I saw no one. I started to breathe in and out slower.

Once I was finally able to catch my breath I walked slowly to the front door and fumbled with the keys in my hands. After what felt like hours, I was finally able to turn the key in the lock the right way; I unlocked my door as fast as I could. It felt as if somebody was watching me, but when I looked around there was nobody to be found. The street was as quiet as it always was and everything seemed as it should be; normal.

As soon as I was inside, I locked both locks, including the dead bolt, behind me. I leaned against the back of the door and tried breathing in and out. I ran to the kitchen and turned on the faucet, placing my hands under the running water I cupped it so that I could bring it up to my face. I drank the water for a good sixty seconds and then splashed the water on my face. I tried to recollect my thoughts cause this shit didn't feel right. As I thought back, I knew I had remembered to eat and I got some water from Trixie before I got on stage. Something just wasn't adding up and I couldn't put my finger on it, but shit at that moment I didn't even have the energy to care or better yet to think it through.

I took a couple of more deep breaths and headed towards the hallway and into my room. I stripped off every piece of clothing and went straight to the bathroom. I reached inside the walk-in shower grasping for the knob turning it towards me to make the cold water start flowing out. As soon as I stepped in I slid straight to the shower floor with my back against the wall and let the cold water run all the way from my head to my toe. I just sat there for a few minutes, still trying to figure everything out. Finally, I got out to head to bed. I reached for a towel for my hair and my robe. I didn't even feel like changing into shit, I just grabbed my phone out my bag and went to lay across my California King bed. I called Tesea the moment my head hit the pillow. I told her everything that happened that night and she insisted that she'd come over. I knew there was nothing I could say to make her change her mind, so I just agreed and hung up the phone.

Not even 15 minutes later I heard the doorbell ring, I forced myself to get up and look through the peephole to see Tesea's ass standing on the other side. My pooh looked worried as could be, and I hated that she had to get up in the middle of the night to rush over here to me. I unlocked both locks and then the dead bolt to let her in. Tesea wore true religion shorts, a black tank top and some blue and red Jordan's. You could tell her ass just threw something on but Tesea was a thick ass high yellow bone, she looked good in anything and her ass was as big as Texas. She grabbed my arm on the way through the door and started going in.

"Bitch you look like you just had five niggas fucking the shit out of you then left ya ass for dead. You sure ya ass alright?"

"Yeah Tesea. Shit I really don't know what happened, I was just fine before I got off stage."

"Man, I'm telling you what the fuck it sound like," stopping mid-sentence, she slowly turned to look me straight in the face with the most intense glare. "The bitch drugged you if you ask me. Shit I ain't dumb, and it really don't take much to see that shit ain't adding up". She stated as she kept looking me up and down. I got up and walked to the sliding doors in my kitchen and opened them up to get some fresh air.

"She a hater for damn sure, but I just can't see her doing nothing dirty like that, plus I'm good now. I might've just been light headed." I said as I looked around at my small patch of a so-called yard. Tesea wasn't buying it at all and started back at it.

"Well I don't trust that bitch and if you do you fuckin crazy, but I'm gone leave it alone, as long as you alright."

"Yeah bitch I'm alright. Hell, what you mean, I ain't dead. I was just short of breath. I'm straight real shit."

She looked at me crazy then spoke up, "Alright girl, don't get ya G string twisted now." she laughed out loud at herself and looked around.

"You know Troy having a bachelor's party, and I really don't want none of them skank hoes being there. I rather my best friend be there cause I know nothing would-"I interrupted her so quick not caring how rude I came off.

"Girl naw, I don't mean to be blunt but then again I do. The fuck I look like dancing for my best friend husband to be and his niggas. The fuck? Girl you must still be sleep. So what imma need you to do is get ya ass up and go wash ya face then come back, lay down and close ya eyes for at least a good five minutes and think clearly before opening ya mouth."

I laughed at the thought of it and at the nerve of her. This bitch must be out her mind.

"GIRL PLEASE!? At least think about it with ya stubborn ass. I'd rather you do it, for real Kay Kay."

"Girl will you stop calling me that before somebody hear you slut." I laughed so hard that her ass couldn't help but laugh herself for asking such a stupid ass question. I mean damn, did she forget who she was talking to?

"Kayla, I don't know why you don't like your name? It's pretty and it fits you. Seriously, I want you to think about it though, because I trust you with my life girl, plus I want you to keep an eye on him, so things don't get out of hand. Know what I'm saying?"

"Alright girl, I'm gon think about it. You already know me and him don't get along like that."

"Exactly!" We both laughed at the same time.

Tesea decided to go ahead and sleep on the couch for the night so I went back to bed.

Chapter 2

When I woke up the next morning I felt so much better; I was so rejuvenated. It almost seemed like a sign that it was going to be an okay day; maybe even good. I walked out to the living room to see that Tesea ass was already gone. Blankets were balled up on the couch and the pillow was on the floor. *This bitch could've cleaned up behind herself.* I thought rolling my eyes to the back of my head while reaching down to pick up the pillow. I wasn't even mad at her though she probably was running late for God knows what.

I walked back in the room and picked my phone up from the end of the bed and slid it off the lock screen. I went ahead and checked my missed calls, texts, tweets and Facebook messages. I really just skimmed through most of it to be honest. I had a text from Tesea and Trixie and a Direct Message from Kodak on Twitter. All I could do was shake my head attempting not to roll my eyes. An exasperated breath escaped my lips. The man was fine, but his problem was he knew that. He was standing at maybe about 5'10, with a short fade and perfect waves that could make you sea sick. Rolling my eyes as hard as could, I thought about how this nigga had me all the way fucked up to the point shit was crazy.

It was only crazy because you could tell the nigga don't get told no. In his mind he pretty much assumed that I'd be all over his dick like the next bitch and that's exactly where his ass had me all wrong. I went straight to Tesea's text message and instantly bust out laughing because she was stupid as fuck. I had to read it over again to make sure I wasn't tripping, trying to subdue my laughter I read the text out loud this time.

"Bitch, I'm sorry I left without saying bye but Troy ass text me with that bullshit, talking about he got a list of strippers he want to see since I wanted them to be females I knew. So, hoe guess who on the list besides you? Never mind bitch I ain't got time to wait on ya ass to guess lol. Girl its Trixie bitch ass first on the motherfucking list."

I stared at the phone for a few seconds, but I surely wasn't surprised. See you got to give roses when roses were due. She could dance, can't nobody take that from her, plus she was fun size standing at 5 feet exactly. She had a body on her too, no stomach, bubble booty and was the color of caramel. She went by Trixie because she always had a trick for that ass. I ain't knocking her I just knew how she was and who the fuck she is.

Shit like they say, 'a hoe gone be a hoe regardless'. So now, I had no choice but to go ahead and be a part of the bachelor party despite the fact that I wanted absolutely no parts in the shit. Not only did I need to keep an eye on him, but on her ass too.

So, I texted Tesea back and let her know that I got her and to send me the date, time and the venue of where it was going to be held at. Next, I looked at Trixie's text, which wasn't too much of nothing; all it said was, *'We Carpooling to the Party or Nah?'*. I guess she already got word that she was going to be one of the three strippers that was gone be the light of the bachelor party; I didn't even bother to text her back. I went to Twitter instead to see what the Direct Message was all about. It was a video of me from last night's show and the words under the video that said, *'Come with me'*.

Shaking my head, I exited out of the Direct Message and glanced around the room. I wasn't about to reply to that shit either, shit was corny as fuck. As soon as I went to set the phone down it chimed notifying me that I received another DM. Glancing down at the screen I read what it said out loud.

"Maybe we got off on the wrong foot, let me holla at you outside the club ma." I decided to respond.

'You think? Just cause I strip don't mean I'm into that touching shit, and that grimey shit like doing something strange for a little piece of change, I'm not with the shit.'

Within ten seconds I had another DM saying

'My bad ma, won't happen again. But say, what's up with me talking to you outside the club though? That's all I asked baby girl chill.'

I replied as soon as I was done reading it.

'As long as you ain't on that dumb shit, we can speak in a public setting about business only!!'

I was about to set the phone down until he replied back not even 30 seconds later.

'Bet that, meet me at Starbucks then, round 3:30. Make sure you come by ya self shawty. Don't nobody need to know what we got going on ya dig.'

All I said was alright, then went to the kitchen. I took out a carton of eggs and some orange juice, poured myself a glass, sipped on it while I cracked three eggs into a clear bowl. I sprinkled some salt, pepper and seasoning salt for taste into the bowl of eggs than began to beat them. I pulled out my non-stick skillet, I turned my electric stove on medium high, poured the eggs into it and scrambled them around.

When I was done I poured it on my plate and put them on my stomach quick, fast and in a hurry like I was starving. Even though I was finished eating I continued to sit there thinking about how I didn't know what I was about to get myself into. Snapping out of the little zone I was in, I sat all the way straight up and took a deep breath while grabbing my empty plate.

Slowly but surely, I stood up and walked over to the sink and rinsed my plate and cup out at the same time. Not giving a fuck about the dishes not being all the way rinsed off, I went ahead and put them both in the dishwasher then headed back to my room to find something to wear. It was already leaning towards 1 o'clock since I woke up later than usual. I opened the door to my walk-in closet and picked up my gray and black spaghetti strapped dress, a pair of gray and black Jordan's and a gray blue jean vest. Putting the shoes at the end of the bed I laid my outfit for the day on my unmade bed.

Looking over my fit I ended up taking a double glance over the outfit to see if it was to my taste; shit in my head my swag was stupid and original. I headed to the shower and was in there for what felt like an hour just letting the steaming hot water run all over my body before I decided to caress and lather my body with Dove body wash.

The scent of my body wash smelled so much like Heaven; well shit at least to me it did. When I applied it to my skin it felt like I was at the *Pearly Gates*. Maybe I was enjoying it too much, but shit, who wouldn't want to feel that damn clean. Taking my time to finish rinsing the rest of the soap off my body, I reached down and turned the shower off.

I stepped out the shower wrapping myself in a long body towel as I took my body powder out the cabinet at the same time as my Cocoa Butter and my Victoria Secret Perfume. The same order that I took them out of the cabinet was the same exact order that I put everything on. I really didn't give a fuck about how weird the shit sounds, I'm real OCD about shit like that. I hit every spot and then was on to the next which was my makeup.

I really didn't feel like getting all into that, like taking the time to actually beat my face, especially for this busta. So, I just put on some lashes that I ended up having to double up to make long and bold with some black eyeliner as the finishing touch and called it quits.

Quickly putting on my clothes and checking the time all at once shocked to see it was already 3 o'clock. Letting the first thought that came across my mind escape my lips, I said, "I don't even know why I'm rushing really, this man ain't nobody to me."

I guess I just really wanted to see what he was talking about, after all, it was about money. I checked my phone again and sent Trixie a text telling her 'sure'. Wasn't anything more to say but that. I never let that bitch in on anything going on with me. For one, she was a hater and for two, she was a leech.

Another DM popped up on my screen; it read, *'You on da way ma? I'm just now pulling up.'*

Rereading the message, I had to think for a second. *Damn he early.*

I laughed out loud. "Let me find out this nigga good on time." I said to myself.

I replied with a simple, '*Yes.*' Then I made my way out the door after grabbing my over the shoulder coach bag.

*****

I pulled up to the Starbucks and circled around back to park. It took no time for me to spot motherfucker's hiding in the bushes. At first, I was like what the fuck these niggas doing until I seen the lens of several funky ass cameras. Shaking my head, I put on my stunner shades, turned the car off, grabbed my bag and hopped out hitting the alarm on my way towards the entrance.

I didn't see his ass at first; he was nowhere in fucking eyesight. I did a double take around, and just like magic his ass was right there over in the cut with his explorer hat that had the strings hanging down to where he could connect them under his neck. He had on a blue jean vest with a black tee underneath and some cut up blue jean shorts. Trying not to admire him, I lifted my stunner shades and acted as if I had something on the bridge of my nose.

I couldn't even stunt on this black ass nigga; he was too damn fine. But also, disrespectful, I reminded myself. As I was heading towards the table he noticed me approaching and flashed a mouth full of golds.

"Sit down ma, I got you a latte."

I was starting to feel like his ass was gone burn a hole in my face with this long intense stare he was giving me. I pulled out the chair in front of me and sat down.

"I didn't take you for a nigga that sits outside drinking coffee."

"That's because you don't know THIS nigga. I ain't like these other niggas; I'm me. One of a kind. That's how I was raised to be, which is myself ya dig."

I just looked at him seeing if he was about to carry on, silence was in the air as I continued to stare. It took this nigga a whole sixty seconds to look me over and sip on his coffee; it smelt like pumpkin spice, I couldn't really tell though.

"No disrespect but that ass in that dress will make any nigga sweat."

I just looked at his ass crazy.

"Aye, I said no disrespect didn't I ma. See there you go, why you got ya guards up ma? I ain't gone bite you," there was a pause, "unless you want me to."

He threw that shit in there real slick like. I started to open my mouth and say something but then he went on.

"My bad, that's just me, you can call me Black."

"Alright Black, tell me how you found me on Twitter?" I asked coolly.

"It wasn't hard, it ain't like ya page was private. Never mind all that luh baby. I was interested enough to find ya, that's really all ya need to know. It ain't Rocket Science shawty." He shrugged his shoulders and I laughed.

"Enough?" I commented while sipping on my latte.

"Yeah, ma. Enough because usually I don't do shit like this."

I must've had a mean mug on my face because he put both of his hands up and smirked.

"Listen to what I'm saying first ma before you bring them little paws out. For one, bitches like to throw things in my mouth, make up shit, and will do anything for a few dollars. So, I try to keep to myself even though that's almost impossible to do since I got signed a couple years ago. You got to understand that a nigga had to clear his circle up cause wasn't nobody with me when I was locked behind them walls. At the same time these niggas and bitches stay trying to front on the block like they was down for the kid. Now I'm the word on these streets ya dig. I told my momma I was gone make it and that's what I'm gone do. That's my first lady, my heart. So, I'm gone keep her straight. See you don't hear me though shawty, I really don't think you do, cause now I'm feeling like Mike Jones ugly ass. Back then they didn't want me now I'm hot they all on me!" He laughed out loud to his self then kept going on, "Shit, everybody want me but you. I'm trying to get to the bottom of that issue."

"Black," I spoke up, "That's nice and all and I hear what you saying but you don't even know me, and I thought we was here to talk about business? "

I could tell this was a side of him that most people around him didn't get to see. I could see him in a whole different light, but I was real funny when it comes to mixing business with pleasure. Plus, since me and Chris broke it off a year ago I wasn't too fond of getting myself involved with any nigga. That nigga right there ripped my heart apart, but it was my fault because that's what happens when a bitch gets their feelings involved. I couldn't fuck with it, ain't no more emotional roller-coasters for me.

"Yeah ma, you right, I was just letting you know what's up, so you could see the real me behind the scene cause I see the way you be looking at me like I'm crazy, I'm not that nigga."

He said while taking another drink of his coffee. I waited a few beats then spoke up

"So, what's this you was talking about last night about private group dances?"

He laughed.

"Check it out ma, we hit every city, different clubs, different scenes, I have different niggas with me everywhere I go. So, it's never the same motherfuckers, I don't let a bitch ass nigga get too close; that's how you get fucked off." He took another drink of his coffee then spoke up and said, "It's a publicity thing ma; every time I go out I show out. Popping bottles, smoking loud, and on that bubbly, I got to stay double cupped up. Check it out though, if you join my team you would make ten bands a night plus whatever money that's thrown ya way. Ma you can't beat that ya dig, so what you think?"

I looked around to see all the motherfuckers looking our way smiling and pointing and I knew it wasn't because of me; it was him. I seen a few flashes go off left and right and tried not to look in the direction of them. Next thing I knew a thick ass bitch came strolling over.

She had to be over 6'5 and she was smiling ear to ear. Then she blurted out,

"I love you Kodak can I get a picture, please?" The bitch sounded desperate, couldn't be me for damn sure.

He looked up and flashed his golds, "Yeah shawty"

Then the bitch handed me the phone. I looked at this whore then at the phone and couldn't do nothing but laugh. I laughed even harder when I noticed this bougie ass nigga didn't even stand up to take the picture. Just threw his arm around her waist as she bent down to his level. Snapping a picture real quick, I literally tossed the phone at her, not giving a fuck if it fell, broke or whatever.

I watched as he sent her on her way. She gave him a kiss on the cheek trying to be cute but instead looked like a fucking weeping willow tree. *Sad ass mutt.*

He laughed as she walked off. I knew I must've been looking crazy cause then he smirked before opening his mouth to speak.

"That's just the way of the game ma."

I laughed so hard I almost choked. "I'm not stunting no female, don't flatter ya self homie."

"Say, what I done told you about that shit. I ain't that nigga and I'm damn show not ya ex nigga or whoever the fuck let ya ass spit out reckless shit. Best believe I ain't that nigga shawty."

Tilting my head sideways I tried not to roll my eyes, "Aye you need to chill out with all that hype you got going on."

"Shit I'm just saying lil Momma, I ain't these niggas you see out here on these streets ya dig? Anyways ma, back to what we was discussing. What you think about that?"

"I'll think about it." I paused to try to gather my thoughts before I accidentally let anything stupid come out my mouth. "I want to check it out first see what it's all about. I'm really trying to be a Video Vixen in the very near future NOT just a stripper with skills in a local ass club."

He looked at me for what felt like forever and a day, then he finally spoke up, "Shit anything's possible with me ma. I can see you on the big screen. Thing is we got to make it all the way to that point. You following me ma? Hell, I wouldn't want ya sexy ass in nobody video but mine and that's how that's gone be. You gone be mine watch what I tell ya shawty. You make me wanna make a believer out of you baby girl."

Licking his bottom lip, he smiled looking dead at me with all his golds shining right in my eyes damn near blinding me.

"Boy boo, I don't know about all that." Trying to play it off I laughed.

"See check this shit out again ma, I aint that nigga that got to stunt to impress no bitch; that shit just come with it. When I say I'm gone make something shake that's exactly what I mean; watch what I tell you shawty. With that said I'm gone leave that there."

I was holding my breath as long as I could to try to keep from laughing in this nigga's face. It took me less than a second to realize that I didn't give a fuck; shaking my head at my own stupidity I made sure to laugh again.

"You think it's funny now, but you gone see ma, believe that." he said then went on to say, "This Friday night I'm gone be performing at club Medusa Dallas, the only three-story club I know that be jumping. So, say, come check me out there, then after lil momma is the VIP party with the dancers. That way you can see what it's all about with ya own to pretty ass eyes shawty. You gone have to let me know if you down, so I can text my manager to have you put on my VIP list so, you can get in and get all the luxuries these other bitches don't get. Yeah ma, feel special."

This motherfucker was just like a light skinned nigga. Nigga was too damn cocky, which seemed to irk my soul more than anything.

I looked down at my phone to see that it was already leaning towards twenty-five minutes until five.

"I'll be there so you can go ahead and tell him what's up, make sure he puts me on the list. My real name is Kayla Monroe."

Kodak placed both of his hands together and began to rub both of them together, front and back swaying his hands side to side smirking at me.

"Sexy ass name for a sexy ass stallion. I like that better than ya stage name ma. I'm gone hit him up and let him know what's up, in the meantime can I get the digits, so I can have a better way of contacting you."

"Yeah, as long as you don't be giving it out to ya niggas "

"I don't share what's mine!" he said harshly.

He said that shit so strong that I almost believed I was his. All I could do was shake my head and write my number down on a napkin. As I was getting up he wrapped his hands around my waist and whispered in my ear,

"You will be mine ma, all mine. I'm gone taste every part of you."

Every part of my body started aching, a feeling I ain't felt in over a year. I could feel the moisture in between my legs, but he was never going to know that; at least not that damn easy. I whispered back into his ear,

"We gone see".

I was about to walk off until I realized he grabbed a handful of my ass about to slap the fuck out of as it jiggled in his hand. My mind told me to go off on this mark ass nigga, but my pussy was pulsating and liked the feeling. I could feel every inch through his shorts on the front of my dress, and my ass wasn't wearing any type of panties. He kissed my cheek and told me he'd see me Friday night. I walked away after that, glad to get away to catch my breath, I made a mental note to myself to never let that nigga get that damn close again. He knew what the fuck he was doing, and I knew my ass had to keep my distance, make this shit about money and money only. I got in the car and drive straight home. I was ready to go home and hop my ass right back in the shower because I had to rub this feeling off of me; he got close this time but never again.

******

After I got out the shower I laid across my bed, glad for it to be one of my days off. I reached on my nightstand and picked up my phone. I had over 100 mentions of me on twitter, over 50 unread messages on Facebook and 30 new text messages, and 23 of them was from Trixie. I checked out her messages because if a bitch hitting you up like that then it must be important. As I was scrolling through the messages, I discovered she didn't want shit, not a bitch ass thing. They all were duplicate messages saying the same thing with only two words that said, *'really smh'.*

I'm thinking to myself like what the fuck this bitch talking about? So, instead of replying, I clicked open my twitter app to see my mentions. One read, *'little ole kay coming up in the world'.*

The next one read, *'she ain't gone be nothing but a gold digger'.*

At that, I had to go see what all the damn mentions were about, cause I didn't know half of these motherfuckers. A bitch had me fucked up. I made my own bread and paid my own bills while they sitting at they momma house sharing a damn room with the next motherfucker! I can't stand an in house welfare hoe; I call it like I see it.

When I finally worked my way all the way up to the top I could see what the fuss was about. It was a picture somebody took of me and Kodak while he was whispering in my ear with my ass in his hands. I gasped. No wonder Trixie ass was blowing me up, so I texted her and told her it wasn't nothing like that. We were discussing business. Although I really didn't owe her any type of explanation cause in all actuality I know what really happened that night at the club; I just never busted her bubble. I went back to twitter and went to Kodak page to see if he posted anything stupid. All I did was laugh when I saw the last update was 30 minutes prior stating, *'Momma always said I can have anything I put my mind to.'*

He had over 11 thousand comments. Smiling to myself, I just got off Twitter and called it an early night.

*****

It was Friday before I knew it and I had Tesea's eager ass come with me to the club, so we could see everything in action. We wore matching outfits from head to toe. We were the type of bitches other bitches wished they could be. We had on hot pink high waist shorts with white cut-off half shirts that stopped right below our breast and some white and pink airdates; we checked ourselves twice in the mirror before we headed out.

The club was only an hour away and that bitch was packed. We stood in line for a second until my dumb ass remembered I was on the VIP list with a plus one. Bitches eyes were rolling in the back of their heads cause their niggas necks was breaking trying to look at our asses. We made it inside and heard the DJ blaring Future's *Codeine Crazy*. We made our way to the bar, ordered two patron shots and made our way to the VIP area.

All we seen was ass bouncing everywhere. Shit if that was all I had to do it would be easy money; real quick. We sat to the far left on the couch and waited for Kodak to come to the stage and when he finally did he was up there for a good 45 minutes making them bitches sweat they weaves out. His ass did sound sexy as hell up there; he killed it if I did say so myself.

Me and Tesea went out to the dance floor when he was done performing to show the ratchets how it was really done. Out the corner of my eye I could see Kodak in the VIP lounge looking dead at me, then I saw one of his little fees come and hop on his lap. He didn't even look at the bitch, he was too busy flashing his grill looking at me and Tesea .

The next song that came blaring over the speakers was *Pop That* by French Montana,

"WORK, WORK, WORK, BOUNCE, WHAT YOU TWERKING WITH"

I decided to put on a little show for him and all his friends. I climbed up the ramp by the DJ booth and let my legs spread all the way out like I was doing a split in the air and held myself up with my arms and started bringing myself up and down moving my left cheek then right cheek to every beat of the song. I pulled my legs together on the ramp and started popping and vibrating, then came back down a few steps and used one foot to push myself backwards into a black flip and came down in a split and vibrated my cheeks out of control.

When the song was over I got back up to see all the niggas and females standing around me cheering and shouting like they were giving me a standing ovation. I saw out the corner of my eye that Kodak was no longer sitting down with the lap dog on him, he was standing at the front of the VIP section clapping with his golds shining. I bent over, made my cheeks jump and looked in between my legs, blew him a kiss through the middle of my legs, came back up and grabbed Tesea's arm then rushed off to the restroom.

******

"Biiiiiiitchhhh, ya ass is crazy! Who the fuck was you out there showing ya whole natural ass too?" she said laughing loud as hell, all the lil hoes in the restroom start giving us the stank eye. They were just some hating hoes that needed some dick in they life. I laughed reaching for the paper towel dispenser, yanking a piece of, I dabbed my forehead to get the sweat beads off then said.

"Girl, I'm not 'bout to play with you, you know how I get down!"

"Girl bye, you know you don't be climbing on shit when we go to a club, you save that shit for work and work only!" she laughed and then got a paper towel for herself, so she could dab her forehead. She went on to say, "See you feeling a whole lot better than the other day, I'm telling you that trick had something to do with that, and on top of that Troy ass really gone put her ratchet ass on the list. Please tell me you made up ya mind, please be captain save a hoe for the night cause bitch I would hate to shut the whole mother fuckin shah bang down! "She looked so damn serious I couldn't help but to go ahead and say yeah.

I knew she trusted Troy, she just didn't fuck with that that trick Trixie, shit everybody and they damn grandmama knew how she got down.

"Ugh, girl I got you only because you the bestie, I'll keep my eye on shit and smoke a couple of blunts but as far as taking my clothes off, I ain't gone be able to do it out of respect for you, I'm gone wear something to leave something to the imagination, but trust and believe me bitch ain't shit gon' go down while I'm around!"

"YES!!!, Thank the Lord, girl I knew you would have my back! It's supposed to be next Friday, but if you got to work I can have him change it till Saturday. "

"If I do have to work I can see what I can do about getting my schedule changed."

"You don't have to do that bitch, shit that's the least I could do is work around your schedule, I'm just gone tell him to have it on Saturday because I know you off"

"Alright girl where is it going to be? In town or out? "

"You already know he don't want to do shit in the city, he talking about Las Vegas only because what happens in Vegas stays in Vegas!"

" BLAH, you know my ass gone tell you everything even if ya ass don't want to hear it, now bitch let's get out of here and go home, it's hotter than a fat monkeys coochie right now."

"Let's go!" she agreed.

We headed for the door, as soon as it flung open, there Kodak ass was standing with his hand over his designer belt and a double cup in his hand. Shit smelled so strong and fruity. I was almost tempted to grab the damn cup myself and take a slug. He was just grinning, golds were just flashing and the females in the background was going crazy. He took a slow sip from the cup, and licked his lips then said,

"Sup ma, I see you was doing ya thing out there. You think about what we talked about?" I giggled for half a second.

"Yeah, I'm down, you got the number, me and Tesea was just bout to bounce." I grabbed her arm to make sure I didn't fall for his smooth ass mouth, Tesea knew I had a thing for them hood niggas, but they wasn't no good.

"Fa shoo ma. Imma hit you up and let you know what the play is. Sure enough Imma have something coming up here soon."

"You do that."

I walked around him pulling Tesea along with me until I felt a tight ass grip on my ass. I tried to turn my head but Kodak ass was right beside me kissing my neck, he came up to my earlobe and nibbled on it a little bit, I could feel Tesea eyes burning in the side of my head. I could only imagine what the fuck was going through her head. My train of thought was cut off when Kodak started whispering in my ear,

"Remember what I said ma, it won't be long, I know you feeling a nigga."

I could feel my pussy getting wet all over again; I had to get the fuck away from this nigga. All I could say was,

"I heard you; we gone see"

I walked off yanking Tesea beside me. I glanced back over my shoulder to see females surrounding him pouncing aroun , while he just stood there holding his double cup in one hand and the other on his belt grinning. I could see his eyes shining thru his shades. I turned back around as we made our way through the crowd and through the doors. It felt so good outside as it started to mist just a little.

I was so happy to get the feel of fresh air that I almost just wanted to stay standing there in that same spot washing the sweat off my body with the mist and wind. Tesea couldn't help herself, she just had to speak up and I knew it was coming.

"Now I see why ya ass was showing out, that nigga trying to put his self on ya brain and it's working! Girl hold up, ain't that the same nigga Trixie ass said raped her, Kayla don't get caught up with the bullshit."

We started to head toward the parking lot looking for where we parked the car at.

"Tesea, you know that nigga didn't rape nobody, why would he? Look at the females that be all up on his dick!" I laughed a little then continued, "Plus bitch I ain't told nobody till now, but I was there, I left my phone in the back and found Trixie ass acting a fool sucking dick to the bone, long story short she was mad cause that niggas dissed her ass like something serious "

All Tesea could do was shake her head in disbelief as we got in the car.

"I always knew that hoe wasn't shit but damn that shit take the cake. That shit so foul, she fucking with somebody life!"

"Girl I know, that's why I don't fuck with her now."

We drove the rest of the way in silence, I leaned over and gave her a hug as we pulled up in front of her house, then drove off. I made it home to see another car in my driveway and I know didn't nobody know where the fuck I stayed. My heart felt like it was beating through my chest, I sat in the car for a second thinking about if I needed to pop the trunk on a motherfucka real quick.

I'm a very private person, nobody knew we're I lived at, not even my ex after I moved because the pain was too real for me, so I kept to myself. My business was my business, I didn't have to worry about nobody but myself. I've learned to be very independent, not needing a nigga for shit. I tried to look through the car's window, but the windows were dark as fuck I don't even see how the mother fuckas was driving. I'm gone have to get a alarm system, I thought instantly.

I was hesitating on getting out of the car, so I tried to focus my eyes on the car in the drive way to see if I knew anybody that drove something like that. It was a blue and black Camaro with some big ass rims and the windows was dark as fuck. I kept running through my mind trying to see if I could remember anybody with that kind of car. I kept coming up empty.

It seemed like my heart was going to burst racing faster and faster, then again it could be the patron.

I didn't like this feeling, but I was going to try my luck anyway to see what the fuck was going on and who the hell would be at my damn house at this hour. I turned off the car and slowly picked up my things from the passenger seat with my eyes still on the car in front of me. I opened the door and got out. It didn't even seem like anybody was in the car and that was weird as fuck.

I was heading to the door bout to call the cops in case a nigga tried to rob me until I heard a voice on the door step.

"Damn, you gone leave a nigga waiting ma?" it was Kodak.

CHAPTER 3

I felt anger build up inside of me I was confused and shocked at the same damn time. First of all, how the fuck this nigga knew where I stayed at and second of all, how the fuck this nigga beat me to my own damn house? He was just standing on my front porch looking like he belonged there, and my ass was just stuck there looking dumbfounded. He stepped down off the porch and walked over towards me.

It felt like my legs were rubber and my feet were glued to the ground; I couldn't move let alone breathe. I was just trying to get through my mind if this shit was real or not, I just didn't understand. I looked down to see if my feet were really glued to the ground and when I looked up he was right in my face he spoke so smooth and low that I almost didn't know what he said.

"So, you gone let me in ma?"

I stood there for what felt like forever and felt the heat rise in my body.

"Nigga how the fuck do you know where I stay in the first place? Tell me, before I call the laws on ya ass."

"Chill out ma, just know I got my ways, I didn't come outchea to start no problems ain't no need to get pigs involved, I borrowed my partner car, so I could sneak away and come to you ma."

"That don't explain how you found out where I live at, shit ain't adding up to me."

"Chill ma, let that shit ride, you gone let me inside or nah?"

"Should I?"

"Stop tripping shawty." He led me up to the porch like he owned the motherfucka.

"You gone unlock the door?" He stood there looking me dead in my eyes

"Shit I'm trying if you'll give me time."

He didn't say anything, he just leaned against the brick wall and waited, watching me through his shades and sipping his double cup. I pulled my keys out and was looking at him out the corner of my eye. There was just something about him I just couldn't figure it out.

As I was pushing the door open I could feel his arm wrap around my waist while his other arm was in the air holding up his double cup, the way he was wobbling behind me was like his pants was about to fall down. He closed the door behind him while his phone started going off, he reached in his pocket while I turned around to face him with my arms crossed over my chest.

He put the phone up to his ear and said, "What's up, shawty?"

I thought that shit was so disrespectful. He was reminding me of all the reasons of why I can't fuck with him he went on to say

"Nah." I could hear a bitch yelling in the background over the phone

"Bitch I'm busy, say you already know you ain't shit to me man, I'm trying not to hurt ya feelings ya dig." *This dirty little dog,* I thought to myself shaking my head.

"Aye, say don't try to threaten me with no shit, I ain't tripping on nothing I'm sipping on something and I got a bad bitch in front of me ya dig, I'm out."

I looked at him like he was fucking crazy, I know it couldn't've been me on the other end of that phone, cause a bitch like me would've jumped through the damn phone on his arrogant ass. He sipped on his cup while he put the phone back in his pocket, I sat down on my velvet leather couch while he stood up looking like he was about to tip over.

"It look like you got some business to tend to, I don't need one of ya fees to get mad about you stalking and following my ass around." He laughed out loud.

"I didn't follow or stalk you ma, apparently you want me here as much as I want to be here."

"Boy, you don't know what I want-" I spoke up, but he chimed in before I could finish my sentence.

"You wouldn't've let me in Kayla."

"Don't call me that!"

"Shit that's ya name; I'd rather call ya by ya name than yo stage name, that's tacky ma, but we ain't got to get into that right now." with that being said I snapped back,

"Don't you got a bitch to tend to?" He laughed at my anger,

"Ma you tripping, that's how I know you feeling a nigga, that bitch wasn't ever shit to me but a fuck, but you ma, you gon' be everything, watch what I tell ya now." he paused for a second, "That ass had me hypnotized from jump and I couldn't help but to put that big jiggly thang in my hands, you know how to get a nigga dick on rock."

Looking up at him still standing over me I said, "That's my job Black, but I don't have control over any nigga's arousals."

"Stop playing ma, you been knowing what that ass been doing to me." He sat his cup down on my end table and grabbed my hands to pull me up. "Come on ma, show me were ya room at, let's lay down and talk for a minute."

I looked into his shades while he licked his lips, looking at my reflection, I looked like I was about to jump this nigga bones , I had to relax my mind and try not to think about it.

"Nigga you don't want to talk."

He cupped his hand under my ass and said, "Maybe not, sounded good though didn't it?"

He pulled me close to his body. I could feel his dick through his pants, shit felt like an anaconda, I lost all sense of mind and turned around grabbing his hand that was originally on my ass and led him to my room.

Kodak slapped my ass then stood back and watched it jiggle, I turned around to see him grinning ear to ear. I still can't believe this nigga was in my room, in my house, in my face. At this moment it really didn't matter though, I could feel myself giving in. Shit I already had when I opened up the door. Even though I was still confused on how he found out where I lived at, it was like at that moment it didn't matter either.

He moved around me, knocking off my train of thought, he sat on the bed and kicked his shoes off like it was his bed, like he just knew he belonged right there at this moment. My heart was starting to race again, and my mind started to jumble around; nothing seemed clear, I was just living in the moment.

Kodak took his pants off looking dead in my eyes through his shades, he placed both hands behind his back leaning backwards on the bed without laying down. He tilted his chin up in a motion that was telling me to come here. I just stood there for a second, staring at his rock-hard erection with the tip of his dick poking out the top of his boxers. I couldn't lie, that motherfucka looked like it was at least 11 inches long, he had my pussy jumping up and down inside my shorts and I could feel the waterfall from my lips seeping down the sides of my inner thighs.

I walked a half step over to the bed and climbed on top of him, without saying a word he sat up a little bit and pulled my shirt off over my head. Since I didn't wear a bra my 34 ds bounced out with my nipples hard and sensitive. He rubbed his thumb over both nipples and then stuck his thumb in his mouth to get it wet and then rubbed his thumb back over them. All I could do was let out a small moan. That dick felt so good even with my shorts on, I could feel it throbbing underneath me and I could feel it growing harder and harder.

In that instance, he put his whole mouth around my left titty and started sucking it like it was a baby's bottle, he moved over to the next one and nibbled it a little bit then went around my nipple with his tongue flicking the other nipple with his index finger, making it harder and harder. He traced his hand up my back up to my neck and reached up to my hair and pulled down on it making me lean my head all the way back and started kissing me from my belly button , up to my neck .

He kept his hand wrapped around my hair and said, "Damn, that pussy wet ma."

He used his other arm to wrap around my legs and lifted me off the bed. *This nigga is strong as fuck,* I thought to myself. He turned me all the way around with his dick poking at my shorts, he laid me on the bed and took his boxers and shirt all the way off. But I could see this nigga still had left his socks on, I started shaking my head. Kodak stood there admiring my body stroking his dick that looked like it was as long as a damn yard stick. This nigga had his dick in his hand and his shades over his eyes smirking. When he came over to the bed he nearly ripped my shorts off with one yank. I unbuttoned them and slid them down so that I was naked as hell. My pussy was throbbing, that dick looked like a gold mine; I had to have it. I reached my hand into my pussy and brought my finger back up to my mouth and sucked on them looking straight at him while he was stroking his dick.

His golds flashed at me, so I reached my hand back down and started playing with my clit.

Kodak moved so swiftly and removed my hand from over my pussy lips and got on his knees lifting my legs up in the shape of a V. His tongue made circles around my clit, he nibbled on it and sucked every bit of juice out of me. He came back up and pulled me upwards and stood over me. He slapped my lips with his dick and started stroking it to were pre cum was dripping out. He reached for the back of my head and pulled it closer to the tip of his dick. My mouth flew open; I sucked on the head of his dick and slowly licked my way to his balls, I took my hand and held his balls in my hand caressing them. Kodak slowly pulled his dick out my mouth and grabbed my hair with a tight grip and eased his dick back in my mouth and slowly started fucking my mouth. Every stroke he made he groaned, next thing I knew I was flipped over in a milla second with my ass cheeks spread apart, while he licked in and around my hole. I never thought I could be so damn turned on by a nigga I knew just wasn't shit.

He put the condom over his dick that he got out his shorts pocket and entered my pussy without warning going at a steady pace. I could feel every inch of him around every corner. I grabbed the comforter which made him go harder, he reached to remove my hands and said, "nah ma, bring that ass here, pussy feel tighter than a virgin's." he smacked my ass and flipped me over pulling me on top of him.

I hopped off his dick and stood up over him, I immediately slid down in the splits backwards to wear my ass was sitting on his stomach and I was riding his dick like a cowgirl while he had both hands on my ass. I vibrated my ass cheeks making him slap them then squeezed harder until he shot hot cum into the condom. I raised myself up with my legs trembling so hard I could barley move. I seen him stroke his dick a little more to get the rest of the cum in the condom. I laid back on the bed while Kodak reached for his phone and headed to the bathroom and closed the door behind him. All I could hear was the water running, then all I could think about was that dick and how it even got that far. It was too late now; I already let him hit it, taste it, spank it. The whole damn 9 yards. I couldn't believe myself ; the toilet flushed and the door flung open. Kodak was hanging up the phone probably with one of his fees or the same one he puked out a couple of hours ago. His dick was still rock hard in front of him, and I just noticed this nigga still had on his shades the whole damn time.

"How them guts feeling ma?" as he was talking he was looking around on the floor for his boxers, this nigga was full of his self.

I just giggled, "I'm good, you bout to bounce right?"

"Yeah ma, I got to return my partner car, we gone have to link up, you know I ain't bout to let you go like that. I might have ya ass stop stripping fuckin around with me, especially since a nigga done tasted that berry, ah yah ma that's mine and I ain't gone play with ya ass behind it!"

This nigga could not think I was gon be taking him seriously, the dick was good, shit matter of fact it was damn good, but one thing that nigga was never going to know was that. The nigga was feeling himself like always. What the fuck have I got myself into? I had this strange feeling that it was about to be some shit from here on out.

"You feeling ya self ain't you?"

"Nah ma, but I'm feeling you, I got to jet though and give this nigga his whip."

He pulled his pants up, put his shirt over his head and stood back, looked at me and flashed his golds then leaned over and kissed my nipple which made my whole body shake. He felt it, leaned up and for the first time pulled his shades down to show me his gray eyes. They were so beautiful, I was breath taken, he put his thumb under my chin and pulled my face leveled to his and gave me a kiss so sweet that my juices ran down my inner thighs yet again. Kodak pulled his head back and winked at me causing me to shudder.

"Alright ma, Imma catch up with you." with that he was gone like the wind, I heard the door close behind him and the car start up. I got up and slipped my robe on and went to lock the door.

******

CHAPTER 4

I woke up the next morning feeling refreshed and so stupid at the same time, I didn't even wanna think about it. I just laid there for the longest time trying to get my mind together. My body felt so tingly all over that I didn't even want to move. I rolled over to see that the window was wide open, blinds was open and the curtains were back. I forgot to close them before I went out last night, there was too much going on. Ugh, it was no big deal though somebody probably got a free show, but I hoped not.

I rolled out the bed and went to the living room to look for my phone. I found it laying on the couch where it all started at, I picked it up to see there was 3 blocked calls and a whole lot of messages and mentions. I scrolled through them, not really thinking much of them. I saw that I became an Instagram star overnight, motherfuckas kill me; I already knew it was only cause of Kodak. A lot of niggas posted the video of me in the club and it had over 30,000 retweets. I shook my head and laid the phone down and picked up my keys because I knew I forgot to lock the car. When I opened up the door, I almost passed out, my windows were busted, and all four tires were flat, the words 'sloppy seconds hoe' was written all over my car with spray paint.

I dropped to my knees clutching my phone in my hand, I was appalled that not only one person knew were I stayed, but apparently other motherfuckers did too. This shit was crazy! I couldn't believe my eyes, like who the fuck would take the time to do this shit. I worked so hard to get this car all on my own. Not knowing what else to do I let the tears flow down my face and texted Tesea telling her to come over asap. She would know something serious would've had to happen for me to text her some shit like that. She was always by my side when I needed her; she kept me afloat. I just didn't understand how the fuck I couldn't've heard my own windows breaking. *Was I fucking or sleeping at the time*, I thought to myself. I just didn't know.

Shit was getting too crazy and too fast. I was starting to think maybe one of Kodak's fees followed his ass but I got to second guessing myself because I didn't see how. When I looked around last night I didn't see anybody but the car in my drive way. Shit wasn't adding up, my mind was too gone to even try to pull together an idea of what could've possibly happened. I seen Tesea pull up and park behind my busted up car in Troy's Ford F150, his white boy truck, as I called it. She hopped out with the quickness after turning the truck off. She rushed to me, I was still in the doorway on my knees in disbelief.

"Bitch what happened?! Oh my God, oh my God, are you okay?"

I just looked at her with my eyes red as fuck.

"Come on, girl we gone have to get you inside, so we can file a police report, your insurance should cover it."

She sounded so sure, it wasn't like I couldn't make the money in a couple of nights to get all the damages repaired; it was the principal of it. It was the first real thing I ever did for myself; it was my ticket to independence.

"Who would do something like this?" I said in between sobs.

"Probably that bitch Trixie"

"You know nobody know where I stay, especially that hoe."

"I'm sure that bitch had a way of finding out, this nigga already don't sound like good news, you might want to stop while you ahead boo."

I was trying figure out why she said that but at that moment I didn't care, I knew she was right, she always was.

We called the cops and filed a police report, I had to go with Tesea to catch a ride to work later on, I just had a feeling this wasn't the end of the bullshit. I packed a small bag and we were on our way.

****

After Tesea dropped me off for work later on that night it was like I was there but wasn't at the same damn time. My mind was in so many places when I was on stage, I didn't half do it, never that, I was always a bitch about my money, it just wasn't the same. When I finished I went back stage to the locker rooms.

I found Trixie's monkey ass in the chair next to my shit, it took everything in me to not accuse her of the shit that happened to my car.

So instead of accusing her I just simply asked, "What you do last night heffa?" looking dead at her while she pulled up her knee-high boots, wearing no top and a G string.

"Nothing bitch, was with the FAM really wasn't shit to do."

That bitch was lying through her damn teeth. I wasn't going to tell her what happened, I was just gone have to do some digging on my own or just leave the shit alone.

"Humph, I'm surprised I didn't see ya ass at Kodak show at the club and what the hell you run out for the other night?"

"Go for what, I don't want to see that nigga in my eyesight, I'm good I done been down that road, you need to be careful girl"

I rolled my eyes to the back of my head, "Let's not go there Trixie, leave that shit alone."

"I'm just telling it how it is, so what's up with the bachelor's party for Troy, it's on Saturday, what time you coming by to get me so I know ahead of time, it's only a day away now."

"Be ready by 10:30, I got to handle a few things with my car."

"What's wrong with ya car? If you want, we can ride in my car."

" Nah, it's in the shop, it will be out by then, just be ready."

I walked away and packed up my shit for the night, that bitch knew damn well what happened to my car but she played the shit off real good. I was gon get to the bottom of it.

*****

Saturday morning was here before I knew it, Tesea texted me last night and said there was a change in plans that the venue had been changed to the Hilton in town, because their money was looking a little funny at the moment. She even mentioned that the wedding was being pushed back a little just a couple more weeks. *At least it wasn't months*, I thought. I just wanted to see her happy.

*****

I caught a cab to pick up my car from Burnoose on Spruce St., all the Mexicans were washing it down as I arrived at the shop, I was so grateful to see my baby back looking so fresh and so clean.

As I was heading over from the cab to meet the owner he spoke politely, "Hey ma'am, as you see we got your car back looking almost brand new, the rims are a little scoffed but it's barely noticeable, if you follow me we can head inside and get your keys."

I followed behind him feeling blessed as ever, glad to have no sort of hold up because I paid in advance. My car was sitting pretty as hell when I saw it on the lot. When we made it inside the office he went behind the desk and retrieved my keys off the hook.

"Thank you so much I really appreciate it." I shook his hands with both of mine.

"Your more than welcome, I wanted to also mention that there was an envelope left in the car just with your name on it, we put it in your glove box, so glass particles wouldn't get into it."

"Thank you."

As I was walking out of the door heading over to my car I tried to remember if I left anything inside the car that night. I could've sworn that I grabbed everything out the car, and never left any type of mail in the car, even on my worst days. Hell, who knows though I haven't been acting like myself lately. So, shit anything was possible at this point. I thanked all the Mexicans surrounding my car and they blew kisses as I got in and started the car.

I reached in the glove compartment as I was driving off expecting it to be a old bill, instead it was a blank envelope that had my name spelled out in black sharpie, putting it down I just figured I'd wait till I got to the house to open it. I couldn't remember but was suddenly very sure I didn't receive no shit like that in the mail, I was having a dumb ass blonde moment. There wasn't even a damn stamp on the envelope; shit was just getting crazier and crazier by the second. I pulled in the driveway to see my house and drive way empty as I left it. "Thank God!" I said out loud, I didn't need any popups, surprise visits or whatever you wanted to call them. Since the shit was racking my brain I turned off the car, turned down Kevin Gates Posed *To Be in Love* and reached over and picked up the envelope.

Opening it was easy or whoever wrote it didn't really seal the envelope to where you had to rip it open to get inside. Once open, it read one sentence in some pretty ass cursive, the handwriting looked familiar I just couldn't remember where I'd seen it before. I stared long and hard at the one sentence on the paper, reading it over and over in disbelief. I read it so much that the words just started to flow out my mouth.

"If you don't leave him alone, you and him both are going to weep what you sow."

I balled the paper up turning on the car at the same time then turned it right back off again because I didn't know what I was doing. When I got out of the car I threw the paper in the street and reached for my phone to DM Kodak.

I scrolled to his page and clicked on the direct message at the top of the page. My thumbs moved so fast you would've thought they were gonna fall off. Once I was done typing, I read it out loud,

"Say my nigga, I don't know what you and the next bitch got going on but leave me and my property out of the shit ya dig in yo voice" I admit the last part was petty, but I was serious as fuck.

Not even 60 seconds later he replied back,

'Ma you tripping, none of these bitches got nothing on you, you real funny though with the mockery chill out before I fuck you up myself now Digg that'

I didn't even respond back to the fuckery. Nothing was adding up, and motherfuckers was acting clueless.

Storing the nonsense to the back of my mind I headed towards my room to get my outfit and stilettos out the closet. Placing the phone down on the bed I walked into the closet, reached over for my fit that was hanging up in a clear wrapper. I pulled it down I placed it on the bed, checking my phone it was already eight thirty, placing the phone back down, I took the clear wrapper off my outfit to take another look at it, just to make sure it wasn't too much. Once I had it laid on the bed I stepped back and did a once over.

My colors for the night were silver and pink, I was wearing a lace jumpsuit, completely see through but I had flower kettles to cover my nipples. My stilettos were bright pink and accommodated the outfit perfectly. At first, I was thinking it was a little too much then again this was as modest as it could possibly get for a damn bachelor party that I didn't want to be a part of in the first place. "It is what it is, there was no going back now; I already agreed to it." talking out loud to myself I walked in the bathroom to take a shower.

*****

Nine forty-five exactly I was done with everything, I braided my hair into big goddess braids, applied my makeup, threw on my lashes and my sliver hoop earrings. I looked myself over in my full body mirror placed behind my door and thought to myself that I was a little too fine to be going were I'm going. Tesea's ass knew how I got down though, I could never go out looking like a bum hoe that's a fact; I didn't go all out though. I headed out the bathroom, picked up my phone and the, first thing that popped up on my screen was Tesea text saying,

'make sure them niggas behave tonight' laughing to myself I replied

'Girl calm ya ass down and let ya nigga enjoy his last night of being single'

The next text that popped up was from Trixie saying she was ready, she sent a picture along with her text showing me her scandalous fit for the night. She wore a white and pink lace long sleeve cut off shirt, that stopped right below her titties, she wore no bra underneath and her titties sat upright; I'll give her that.

Her boy shorts stopped right below her bikini line and they were see-through as well, but at least she had enough common sense to put on something underneath it which wasn't much but an extra thin ass G string that was pink and rocked some pink and white red bottoms. She looked straight, well good I guess, it was just a little much. Tesea would be knocking bitches left to right if she seen the shit herself. Thank God she wasn't going to see it though, because I was just ready to get this shit over with and come home to my big ass bed. I texted Trixie back letting her know I was heading out.

When I pulled up to Trixie's apartment building she was already standing outside, bitch didn't even bother to put on nothing over her fit, that's how you know this bitch just wanted to be seen. Pulling up to the curb she opened the door with the car still moving, I got irritated real quick.

"Damn bitch, ya ass couldn't wait till the car stop first?"

"Girl its cold." she was laughing at herself while I was rolling my eyes at the same time

"Girl just get ya ass in the car, you letting my heat out, you should've put on a damn jacket." She got in and closed the door.

"I was rushing bitch, the fuck got into you."

"I'm just ready to get this shit over with."

With that being said I drove off, twenty minutes later we arrived.

Inside the elevator we waited to reach the top floor were the presidential suite was, when we finally made it to room 333, I could smell the loud slipping from under the door and 2 chainz song *I Love Them Strippers* blasting through the speakers. Trixie's extra ass knocked on the door smiling ear to ear. The door swung open and Troy's bright ass was standing in the door way wearing Polo from head to toe with some Gucci flip flops. Tacky as hell in my opinion, but his bright ass was fine, he reminded me of Chris Brown's sexy ass.

He let us in and I could tell he was already drunk. A big alien amazon chocolate bitch was already inside bending over shaking her ass loosely. She was getting it though, I looked around the room and noticed the big ass hot tub, bottles on top of bottles, cameras and a DJ booth. I took off my pea coat and started dancing along with Trixie. Money was flying and blunts was being passed around. Troy came to me and handed me a fresh lit blunt and that was the last thing I remembered.

I woke up in a bed in one of the rooms with a camera in front of the bed. I was confused as fuck ; I looked down and all I seen was blood.

CHAPTER 5

I was in complete and utter shock, I did another glance down to see if it was still there; it was. Was all a dream? My eyes were closed for what felt like hours when I finally opened them. Blood was everywhere, and my vagina was soaked with blood. I reached down there to touch it and suddenly my whole body felt like lightning just struck me. Gliding my hand up over my body, my entire outfit was ripped all over. As I was trying to figure out what happened, I listened to see if anybody was still in the hotel suite. Not hearing anyone I tried to roll off the bed. It was the worst feeling I've ever felt in my entire life. I could see used condoms under the bed, instantly tears started falling from my face, burning my eyes.

I couldn't move at all. I just sat there in shock. I didn't know what to do first. I sat there and cried as I looked around the room. There were empty bottles, blunt wrappers and cigarette butts all over the floor. The room was trashed. I grabbed onto the edge of the bed to pull myself up and limped over to the large ass bathroom that was inside the hotel room. Looking in the mirror had me instantly wishing I didn't. My neck was sore with red marks. I didn't bruise easily either like most black people. My eyes were bloodshot red, and my nipples hurt so bad they felt like they were about to fall off. I turned on the faucet while quickly taking both hands and placing them under the stream, so I could splash water on my face. I came to my senses at the same time the water hit, I needed to get to the hospital ASAP.

I limped over to the camera standing on the tripod and pushed the play button. All I could see was me being thrown onto the bed and some kind of object being put inside of me that looked almost like anal beads, one by one they were going in and out. I watched the video over and over. I could tell that it wasn't the full tape. It was like someone left it there for me, just so I could watch it.

My mind was racing; I felt so numb. I carefully hobbled out of the room to see the hotel suite completely empty. The fuck was going on? I just didn't understand; almost didn't want to. Surprisingly my keys were laying on the counter and my coat was on the floor. I bent down to grab my keys. Turning around, I remembered the camera, I turned around to grab it, I knocked over the tripod and caught in mid air before it could hit the ground My heart began to race again. Limping as fast as I could I grabbed my coat and I hurried out of the room, knocking over cups that were on the desk by the door.

********.

I rammed my body against the shower wall so loud the neighbors could probably hear me; I didn't want to think or feel. When I went to the hospital they performed a rape kit on me and tested me to see if anything was in my system, 2 things were for sure I had been raped and there was more than one drug in my system, ecstasy, cocaine and some sort of date rape drug. Shit was unbelievable. Last thing I remembered was a blunt. I didn't know how the fuck Trixie got home and I didn't know where the hell everybody else went. Shit was so fuckin unclear I couldn't even attempt to recollect it.

My doctor asked me if I wanted to file a police report with the officer, but my hard-headed ass declined. I told the lady repeatedly that I didn't know who could have done it and I didn't remember shit. I felt like she was looking at me like I deserved the shit because of the clothes I arrived in, but maybe she was looking at me out of concern or sympathy. I didn't know what it was, but I didn't like the way she was looking at me. I didn't need sympathy; I needed help, I needed to go home.

****

I was in a daze, I just laid on my bed naked, trying to remember what I could; I kept coming up with blanks. I called my boss at the club to tell him I wasn't going to be in for a couple of weeks because an emergency came up. He told me he was going to see if Trixie could fill in for me for the time being, I agreed. *I'm sure she'll just love this* I thought to myself before hanging up the phone.

I decided to call the bitch, Trixie, myself to see what the fuck was going on without telling her anything to see if she just come out with it and be real from the jump. I scrolled through my messages and found the one from her the night before clicked on her number and waited for her to pick up, she answered on the third ring.

"What's up bitch, what you doing?"

I couldn't help myself from saying, "The fuck you mean what I'm doing. What the fuck happened to you last night?"

"Damn bitch what the hell has gotten into you, you don't remember? Troy friend Andy and them other niggas took me an ole girl with them last night? I ain't, even stunting them not even a bit. I had fun though, me and that girl had an orgy with them niggas. Yo ass was half-sleep, looking dead on the couch, I told you before we left, and you told me to call you when I got home, I forgot, but Troy said he was gone make sure you got to your car safely."

"Oh my fucking God so you just left me there? Anything could've happened you don't do no shit like that!"

"What you mean I left you there, bitch you was high as fuck, you said you was on your way out the door too so what you mad for? You made it home, didn't you?"

"Yeah, bitch I made it home. No, thanks to yo ass please don't ever hesitate to remind me to never go anywhere with yo dumbass again."

I hung up the phone more confused but enlightened at the same time putting 2 and 2 together Trixie said I was high looking sick and dead and that she and the other girl left with them niggas. You would think, since she said I looked sick that she wouldn't leave me there. What female in the right mind does stupid shit like that? I don't care if I hated you, I would never leave you in a situation that could be unsafe

Nevertheless, that left Troy in mind. He was the one who passed me the blunt. Leland didn't even look like he took a pull off the shit and if my memory serves me correct this nigga let me smoke the blunt to myself since I really was just there to watch over shit and he knew that. My mouth dropped at the realization, this nigga had done laced the damn blunt with cocaine, X pills and roofies! I wanted to scream, I debated on whether or not I should call Tesea's ass, I decided it was necessary. She picked up on the first ring as if she was awaiting on me to call.

"Hey girl, what you doing? Me and Troy was just about to go downtown to this new soul food joint! You good?"

"I'm alright, hush! I was just calling to make sure everything was good with you." there was a slight pause.

"Yeah bitch, why wouldn't it be? I've been wanting to try this place out forever now and Troy real sweet ass was willing to take me out tonight. Are you okay girl? You don't sound like yourself and I wanted to tell you how much I appreciate you for doing that for me the last night." hmm little did she know!

"Yeah, I'm alright."

In the back of my mind, matter of fact, in the very front of my mind I couldn't help but to think how the hell could this bastard go out to eat, having the time of his life knowing that he just raped me the night before. I figured it was best to keep my mouth closed because I had no hardcore proof. Hell, the little clip didn't even show a face.

"Girl, enjoy your dinner. I was just checking on you." I ended the call.

How could I tell her when I knew it would break her heart? Especially when I really didn't even know myself. Whoever it was used a condom so there was no DNA left behind when the rape kit was performed. Obviously, the video was missing more than half the footage. I wouldn't even be able to tell what happened because I honestly had no idea how it went down. How could I tell my best friend that her husband to be was more than likely a low down dirty ass nigga, I wouldn't even know where to start.

I couldn't be the one to break her heart after the way the last nigga did her. I never even got a chance to meet him before it was over. She said he was real secretive. She loved him. I could tell she was heartbroken, until she met Troy and I didn't want to ruin this for her. She deserved happiness. I was stuck between a rock and a hard place, and all I wanted to do was lay there in a ball and cry.

Like, why the fuck would he do that? He didn't even like me. Or so I thought. He was pitiful. How the fuck could he sit up there, eating pies, cakes, macaroni and cheese and all the other good shit knowing what the fuck he did. The nerve of that nigga, suddenly, I felt sick to my stomach, wondering what happened to the other half of the video. I knew there had to be more; I was so tired of repeating the same old song in my head, things still weren't adding up! I felt so fucking disgusted with myself, I felt violated as fuck, I guess when motherfuckers knew you were a stripper, they had no respect, thinking all strippers would go for anything.

****

I hadn't been able to move since everything went down, I'd just been laying low inside the house with my phone turned off. I felt like Trill Fam's song Ducked off. The lyrics described exactly how I was feeling.

"I ain't even in the mood, get from round me. I got too much on my mind. I don't need no company. You can hit me on my phone, but I'll probably let it ring. Trying to chill, trying to do my own thing"

I kept singing just that part over and over and wasn't too sure if it was the right lyrics They weren't accurate at all, but oh fucking well, shit I felt like I was close enough. No makeup had touched my face in over three weeks and I'd been laying on the couch, floor and the bed, doing the same thing; looking crazy eating ice cream. Even the ice cream wasn't filling the void in my stomach; I felt empty. Tired of watching love and hip hop in the living room, I forced myself off the couch and started towards the room to lay across the bed, once again. I was starting to get a cramp in my side from sitting in the same position for too long.

Making my way to the room, I could hear my phone going off repeatedly. I guess it turned back on when I finally decided to put it on the charger during my last trip to the kitchen. I started to shake my head at the same time reciting ducked off out loud, yet again. I didn't want to be bothered with no bitch or nigga. I just didn't have the energy to carry on a conversation with anyone. I turned on my side and picked up the phone to see that I had 10 missed calls from Kodak, as low as it seemed I didn't have shit to say to him either. I mean, what was there to really talk about? I couldn't be a part of no dancing or stripping or anything of that nature feeling the way that I did.

The first message read, *I know you see me calling your line.* The next one said, *I stopped by the club last night where the fuck was you at?* The last one said, *you bet not be given my goods to another nigga ma.*

I wanted to respond but I couldn't. His ass was real funny though just thinking about it, "my goods". Little did he know they were damaged goods now. I wondered if he'd still want them if he knew.

*****

The sun was trying to peek through the blinds in my window. I could feel the heat on my eyelids, I didn't want to move so I just rolled over grabbing my phone to check the time. I noticed that I had a text from Tesea saying,

I don't know if I forgot to tell you thank you for the other night. I hope you know how much I appreciate you Pooh bear and I hope you get to feeling better. Tried going by the club but you wasn't in. Big Boy, the manager told me you were sick. I hope ain't nothing going around bitch lol any who call or text me whenever your body allows you to. Love you bitch.

I laughed a little as I reread the message. This bitch went all out just to check on me. That was sweet of her. I'm glad she understood that I didn't want to be bothered. But then again, it would have been nice to see her. But knowing I couldn't lie to her face made it all the better that she didn't stop by. I didn't know what I'd do or say if I saw her right now.

*****

As I was trying to push myself off the bed I smelled moldy ice cream in the empty container on the side of the bed. I had just put it there a few hours ago. There was no way it was already molded. I picked up the container and put it up to my nose to get a whiff of it instantly putting it back down, gagging at the smell of it. I rushed into the bathroom and flew straight to the toilet, hugging both sides. I threw up everything I put in my stomach over the last few days. I stood up and washed my face with water and stood there for a second. I didn't know what the fuck got into me, but this shit wasn't normal for a bitch like me.

Throwing up? Hell, naw! I shook my head. A little chime on my phone informing me that I had an email, interrupted my thoughts. I stared at myself in the mirror for another second, then walked over to the bed and pick up my phone. I clicked on my Gmail account to see that I had an email from some weird server. Against my better judgment, I opened it anyway and it showed a 30 second clip of a woman's hand poking a hole in a condom. Then I saw myself on the bed in the background. When I tried to reply to the email asking who the fuck sent this shit it was instantly rejected, saying that I wasn't allowed to send the email. Now I was furious. I pressed the play button again to watch the thirty second video a little more closely, studying the hand that had the safety pin in it. It didn't look like Trixie's hand but what the fuck did I know. Hell, it ain't like I go around studying other bitches' hands and shit. That don't even sound right and wouldn't look right either if I was doing some weird ass shit like that. Shit was just getting more and more crazy and I was about to lose my damn mind. I've never done anything to anybody to deserve this bullshit that was going on. My head was pounding like somebody was sitting inside my head banging on some damn drums.

I got off the bed and went to the bathroom to look through my cabinets and drawers to see if I had anything to sustain the ongoing heartbeat that sat in the middle of my head. Reaching inside the drawer I found some aspirin and took three dry. Turning on the water faucet I cuffed my hands and brought them under the cold water then slowly up to my mouth to sip the water out of my hands. Not feeling the sudden relief I was looking for, I went back to the bed and laid my ass back down. Not even two whole minutes after I laid down my phone started going off yet again.

"Ugh can I lay down for two fucking minutes before a motherfucker bother me about nothing? DAMN!" I said out loud hearing my voice echoing off the walls.

Kodak was texting me wondering what the fuck was wrong with me and why the fuck I hadn't been answering my phone. I texted him back.

Don't you have shows to tend to?

It surprised the hell out of me when I didn't receive a text back. I was guessing that shit made him fall back. Throwing the phone back down beside me I just laid there looking up at the ceiling asking God why me? What had I really done to go down this road? I wasn't understanding how that was grounds to go through it like this. I was starting to think maybe I wasn't living my life right and that's most likely the reason all this bad luck shit had been following me, even though I had never intentionally done anything to anyone.

****

I must've dozed off, because when I opened my eyes the sun was going down and I felt the sudden urge to throw up. I rushed to the bathroom and hugged the sides of the toilet, yet again. Tears began to well in my eyes. Something wasn't right. I could feel it in my bones. I decided to go to the drug store and get a pregnancy test. I threw on my blue Victoria's secret jogging suit, then put my shades on, even though it was dark outside. I grabbed my scarf and wrapped it around my neck and rushed out the door grabbing my phone and coach bag, locking the door behind me.

When I arrived at the store I loaded a small basket with a variety of pregnancy tests. I paid for all of them in the self-checkout line to be cautious. Nobody could really see me with this damn scarf and shades on. Once all of them were scanned and paid for I fled from the drug store and drove so fast on the way home that I should've been stopped by the police. Turning off the car, I hopped out and made sure the doors were locked behind me. Carefully, I checked up and down the street, to see if anybody was watching me. I unlocked my front door, and quickly shut it behind me. Once I was inside, I leaned my back against the door, and sighed.

I turned around and locked all three locks then dropped everything on the living room floor, except for the bag full of pregnancy tests. I closed the bathroom door behind me as if it really mattered. I lived by myself, so no one would see me but one time I'd been seen fucking in my own bed, so I could never be too damn careful, could I?

I sat on the toilet and pulled the first test out of the bag and took a deep breath all at the same time. After peeing on the first stick I impatiently waited. Three long ass minutes later, I read it.

My heart damn near exploded when I finally read the results. It couldn't possibly be true, not me! I couldn't possibly be pregnant. I started to panic. I knew it couldn't be right, so I tried to get my breathing under control and took another one, then another one, and then another one. When the bag was empty I realized I'd taken them all and they all said the same thing! What the fuck kind of cruel shit was this, why the fuck would this be happening to me? Me of all fucking people! I didn't deserve this shit! Crying uncontrollably, I didn't know what to do or say and I wasn't sure if anything would come out even if I did try to say anything. My throat was closing up on me and my mouth nor my body would move. Shit was really hitting the fan. It seemed like I was getting hit left and right, blow after blow, all in a short period of time. I threw every single pregnancy test in the trash, one by one. Something had to be done. My best friend was supposed to marry this trifling ass nigga!

This nigga didn't have a heart or soul. He must've already been dead on the inside to pull some foul ass shit like this. I couldn't possibly tell Tesea right off the back. She would believe her man over me, they were supposed to be in it for the long run. Right about now I could kill his ass my damn self. Not knowing what else to do I laid across the bed and closed my eyes. What the fuck did I look like coming to Teasea with some half-truths; all I had was speculations. Not hardcore evidence, just short ass video clips that didn't show nobody but me and a damn hand. On the first video all it showed was anal beads being shoved in and out of my ass. Who the fuck was gon' believe me? The shit sounded crazy as fuck and I was starting to go crazy my damn self. I opened my eyes and closed them again praying to God that he fixed all the wrong things going on with me.

****

The next morning Big Boy D texted me trying to see how many more nights I was going to need off because he was starting to lose some of his best clients that came into the club every night to see me, specifically, twerk something. Texting him back all I said was, *I need a couple more nights and I'll be back promise.* He texted back saying, *Fa sho shawty, make sure you hit me up if you think it'll be sooner than that. You know we need ya ass hurry up and get better shawty.*

Placing my phone down beside me, I had to think of a plan real quick. I couldn't tell Tesea, because I didn't want our friendship tainted. I knew she was probably waiting to get pregnant her damn self. She once told me that she got pregnant with a nigga that she was once dating. Somehow, she had a miscarriage. This baby wasn't for me; it was for her. I knew damn well there was no way in hell I could keep the baby. For one it would be more than wrong of me, I could not bring myself to have this baby, it would hurt me more than anything. It wouldn't only be wrong, but I knew I wasn't ready, especially not like this. The circumstances were all the way wrong.

The timing, how it happened, shit everything. Shit I was not about to be the cause of her heartbreak, she did not deserve the bullshit and I'm sure she wouldn't keep the child that her soon to be husband forced into her best friend. I mean shit if the shoe was on the other foot I know for a fact I wouldn't be able to take on a baby that wasn't mine. I knew she would suffer every time she looked at the baby and I didn't want her to go through that shit, she shouldn't have to. So, I decided to be brave and do something I said I would never do if I was ever to become pregnant. Due to the circumstances I had no choice it was either get a abortion or lose my best friend to some bullshit I had no control over. It hurt me to say I had to get one.

****

The next morning I pulled out my Apple MacBook, and went to the google search engine to look up nearby abortion clinics. Scrolling through the list I found one pretty close to where I stayed at, only a couple of miles away, a place called Discrete Abortions. *Wasn't too discrete by the name*, I thought putting the information in my phone's gps. I got my purse and headed out locking the door behind me. When I made it there I hesitated to get out, the place looked rather scary in my eyes, but that might of been because of the white folks standing outside of the building with their signs, walking in circles chanting shit. I happened to catch a glimpse of a few of the signs, one read

"BABY KILLERS" another one said, "HOW TO KILL A LIFE".

The shit was beyond crazy even though there wasn't many of them it was enough of them to make me second guess shit and make my heart race. Staring at the crazy ass white folks stomping around with the signs, I turned off the car and grabbed my sunglasses and scarf. Wrapping the scarf around my face I got out. After the psycho ass protesters seen me it seemed like they all started talking at once yelling,

"You're gonna burn baby killer!" it took everything in me not to turn around and punch one of them motherfuckers dead in they mouth.

Instead I walked a little bit faster towards the building and once inside I slid the scarf off my face. I walked towards the woman behind the counter with the big ass bowl of condoms sitting in front of her face. She gave me a brochure and told me to take a few condoms as well as sign my name on the list in front of her; then everything was a blur.

****

I was feeling so disgusted with myself, I was too depressed to do anything, the doctor told me I might have symptoms of depression but I never thought it would be like this. It had been a whole week and I was miserable but I was glad I did it, it was the right thing to do. I had to apologize to Big Boy because I knew I had told him it would only be a couple of more days. Shit his ass had better been glad it was only a week, if I didn't have bills to pay I would've stayed my ass at home. I made it to the club thirty minutes early and got myself together in the locker room even though me nor my body was up to it. While I was sliding on my stilettos Trixie came up behind me I could see her in the mirror. She spoke first,

"Damn bitch, yo ass went all out, no wonder you was gone ya ass been too busy going viral!" I spun around so fast,

"The fuck you talking about?"

"Don't play dumb, that video of you and Kodak."

Chapter 6

"What the fuck do you mean of me and Kodak???" I stared at that bitch like she had done lost her mind.

"Girl don't get mad at me, I thought you already knew."

"Knew what bitch? I didn't know shit, or I wouldn't be asking you what the fuck you talking bout!"

Trixie just looked at me and laughed like the shit was really funny, flipping her little bob she must've just had sewn in.

My patience was wearing thin, I did not have time to be playing no guessing games with this nothing ass hoe.

"Bitch let me show you, it ain't that serious, I just figured you was trying to get a little fame in you know what I'm saying?"

She slapped her leg clearly tickled thinking that she was real fucking funny. I was about to pull that fucking weave out her damn head, but instead I controlled myself.

"Kodak was at the bachelor party?" I asked suddenly confused, because if that was the case that left even more unanswered questions, that shit couldn't be right.

"Girl nah, the fuck you smoking? This video was just of you and him." she paused for a second then said, "I see you got a lot more out of him then I did, just wait and see he gone try to diss ya ass too."

I brushed that last little sly comment to the side; me and this bitch was clearly of two different breeds.

"Just show me the what the fuck you talking about Trixie."

She smiled a little too cool for me while pulling her phone out of her bra. She went straight to the video, like she done watched it over and over again; nasty ass . The video was close to an hour long, she pressed play and I could clearly see Kodak's dick going in and out of my mouth, I could tell that the camera was pretty far off, I reached over her to stop the video.

"Where did you get this shit from?"

"It was posted on twitter by what looks like a fake page."

She tried to go back to the page but the page had already been taken down. I shook my head as I got up and moved passed her with nothing left to say. I headed to the stage to make my money for the night. Not being able to concentrate because my mind was running in a thousand different directions, even though I didn't give tonight my all I still managed to make over two stacks.

****

When I finally made it home I was able to think clearly, heading towards the kitchen I opened the fridge to start preparing something to eat. Picking up the lettuce, tomatoes, left over bacon strips and corn I layed it all on the kitchen counter and prepared myself a southwest chicken salad using cut up chicken breast I still had in the fridge. Sitting down at my dining room table, I started to think how someone could've possibly caught all that on tape, and I was sure the world had already seen it before it got taken down.

Then I remembered the blinds were wide open that night because my dumb ass forgot to let them down, and honestly wasn't too much stunting them. What the fuck kind of luck was I having, shit was getting out of control and I couldn't keep shit in my grips it felt like. My gut told me that Kodak did not have nothing to do with the shit. Because first of all his phone was in his pants and it didn't seem like he was paying attention to nothing else at that moment in time, he was already leaned the fuck out. I knew now that I was gon have to call him; I needed to know for myself that he didn't know shit about it. I was already a known stripper, now I was for sure gonna be the hoe that they already thought I was and that was a damned shame.

****

The phone rung three times before it went to voicemail and I didn't try calling again because right when I was about to he texted me saying,

'I'm at my show right now ma, Imma hit you back.'

I thought about texting him back but I changed my mind, not even an hour later he texted me back. I guess he wanted to feel like a man of his word; nigga please.

The text said,

'I already heard ma, when you gone let me slide thru so we can talk, my show almost over shawty'

Not in the mood for whatever kind of game he was trying to play, I debated on whether or not to text him back. Against my better judgement I went ahead and texted him back.

'You can come thru when it's over, but not for no piece of ass if that's what you thinking.'

Not even two seconds later he responded,

'Bet that ma, be there around two.'

"Booty call hours." I said out loud shaking my head at the same time, little did he know, I was dead ass serious.

Too much shit had been going down in these last few weeks and dick was definitely was the last thing on my damn mind. I had to make sure that he had nothing to do with all of this bullshit, even though I had a feeling he didn't. I still had to make sure though, just to make myself feel better if only a little bit. This shit didn't start happening until his ass popped up in my life out of fucking nowhere. This nigga was rich as fuck and had lines full of thirsty ass bitches waiting they turn. Nigga had shows to tend to, clubs to appear at and all sorts of other shit. But yet here he was coming out the woodworks fucking with me and suddenly my life gets turned upside down. Just thinking about the shit made my damn brain hurt, my soul was fucking tired, I was too young to be feeling so damn old.

CHAPTER 7

Two a.m. rolled around and I still hadn't received a text from Kodak's ass, so I went ahead and started turning off the lights. As soon as I was turning off the living room light I heard a loud ass horn outside. I checked through the blinds to see a big ass stretched hummer with Kodak standing outside of it in all black and gold Versace, some gold Versace loafers and his favorite damn shades on. Even in the dark I could still see his golds shining so brightly. I closed the blinds, went back to my room and threw on my Pink jogging suit and zipped my jacket, picking up my keys and phone on the way out the door.

Locking the door behind me, I walked down the driveway towards Kodak; as always this nigga had his double cup with his drink in his cup. He put the cup on the ground right beside his loafers and embraced me grabbing nothing but ass while his arms were wrapped around my waist.

"Boy I thought I told ya-"

"I know what you said ma, shit I can grab what's mine, you should know damn well I can't help myself, look at the way that ass sitting in them sweats sheesh! You ready though?"

"Where we going nigga?" I said grinning, his ass was so sexy I couldn't resist it.

"Don't worry about that ma, you said this wasn't a booty call right? Right, so baby we gone ride that alright with you?"

Instead of saying anything I just pulled my hood over my head and waited for him to open the door. He reached down and picked up his double cup off the ground and opened the door waiting for me to get in. As I was trying to get in this nigga took it amongst himself to cup my ass to help me inside, I swatted at his hands laughing as I landed on the leather seat. The inside was so luxurious my eyes bulged out the sockets trying to capture all the beauty. It looked like a top floor suite at an expensive ass hotel in Las Vegas. Four long leather seats surrounded the sides with a Jacuzzi sitting in the dead middle of the Hummer floor. Bottles surrounded the sides of the Jacuzzi, all different types to choose from, Cîroc, Hennessy, Bombay and so much more. A big screen covered the front of the hummer with one of his music videos playing on it. *This nigga is so full of himself,* I thought to myself, still looking around in awe, there was different color lights shining all over the floor.

"Welcome to my world shawty." he put his arm around me as the car was pulling off.

We cruised the city and all the surrounding areas, popping bottles and listening to his mixtape.

Nigga rapped about some real shit, I could tell that much; it made me wonder about who he was before he became famous.

"I already saw the video ma"

"Then why ain't you tripping, why you didn't do nothing about it?" I stared at him waiting on his answer.

"See me, you don't know what I do, you too busy with ya nose stuck up shawty." stopping his ass right there I could feel the anger boiling inside of me, this shit was his fault, my life didn't start fucking up until this nigga popped up out of nowhere, like a motherfucking ghost or some shit that just wouldn't go away.

"Nigga you don't have to get fly, you the one that popped up at my crib out of nowhere refusing to tell me how the fuck you knew where I stayed at and who-" he cut me off abruptly.

"Ma, you tripping, see you didn't even let a nigga finish before ya mouth started getting fly. Check this out, before ya ass rudely interrupted me I was going to tell you my manager found a way to take it down, I didn't want you to go out like that ma." speechless, I just gazed out the window looking at the city lights as he went on to say, "I don't know a low ass nigga that would do some bitch shit like that. All I know is that it wasn't my end if that's what ya ass thinking, ma we had it taken down as soon as we got wind about it, but hell by that time somebody already sold it to somebody in the tabloids. And I found out where you stayed at from my nigga Chris he said he knew you from a while back."

My heart started racing, I only knew one nigga by the name Chris and that was my ex. *How the fuck does he know Kodak?* I thought shaking my head, I couldn't even speak. I just sat there for what felt like hours before he spoke again,

"What's wrong ma? My nigga already told me he use to fuck with you on that level, me and him use to be cool as hell way back when I was trying to first come up. You just probably don't remember me because I didn't always use to have the nice things I have now or the golds in my mouth. See I been wanting to chop it up with you but I guess you wasn't ready for a real down ass nigga like me yet, Chris ain't fucked up about me wanting to fuck with you. He know his ass really can't say too much of nothing anyway hell. My boy turned out to be fucking with my bitch, which really ain't his fault if she was throwing that cat at a nigga, the nigga was gon be a dog its in his blood. Shit it's in all niggas blood that's just real ma, but the bitch thought I was still gone want her after she let another nigga hit, then on top of that shit the bitch turned out to be crazy as fuck. We ain't gon get into all that right now though, just trust me when I say watch who the fuck ya friends are shawty and who the fuck around you cause everybody ain't ya friend ma trust me, you can't trust no one, that's the realist shit I can tell you. Me and my nigga still cool though, I can't fuck with a hoe with no morals, when you step out with another nigga especially my nigga you ain't shit in my book. I'm sorry but my momma always taught me never let a bitch get the best of you, I ain't gone lie, yeah I was feeling little momma but I had to let that ass go. She got evil ways and as crazy as the shit sound I can feel the shit, I know that bitch still out there lurking, trying to find ways to get me back since I done came up but that shit a no go you heard me."

Everything that he was saying was on a whole nother level and there I was judging him, and I didn't even know him like that. It was a small ass world all I could say was,

"I'm sorry"

"For what ma? The past is the past, I'm trying make you my future, whether you believe me or not, I'm a nigga of my word which means you gone be mine like I said from jump." reaching over he pulled my face closer to his and whispered, "I'm for real ma, you just don't know how much I'm digging you."

****

Before I knew it Kodak was having his driver drop me back off at the house, he kissed me on the neck before letting me out. To my surprise he didn't try anything, didn't try to come in, didn't try to fuck in the back, in the Jacuzzi or nothing. We just rode the night away like we didn't have shit else to do but look at each other, talking about nothing and everything at the same damn time. As I was closing the door behind me Kodak grabbed my arm to say

"Be easy ma, Imma be in touch "

After blowing him a few kisses I went ahead and shut the door. Stepping back, I felt a little closer to him even though he didn't disclose that much information; it felt like enough for now. It felt as if he was opening up to me a lot more than he would if he was around any other bitch.

I watched him have his driver pull off, when they turned at the end of the road I decided to go on inside. Crazy how time flew by when I was around him. When I looked at my wall clock it was already seven o clock in the morning, the sun was hardly in the sky yet.

Deciding I wasn't hungry I went straight to my room, trying to gather everything in my mind first before I completely shut my eyes to the world. Even though Kodak had finally told me how he knew where I stayed at I didn't really like the feeling knowing who had told him. Chris had broken my heart, I mean literally broke my heart, ripped it up into shreds; I never knew a heart could fall apart so fast. When we were together I thought we had a bond nobody could ever break. He was different to me with his big ass Oscar the fish from shark tale eyes. I laughed at the thought of that nigga donut hole eyes. Chris was over 6 ft. looking down on me every time he stood up and was funny when he wasn't trying to be.

I think for the most part that his car made him sexy, driving an all white Crown Vic, windows tinted as dark as they could be with some dice hanging in the window, rims bigger than my lower body. Then on top of that his ass was light skinned, a mixed boy, just pretty with that good ass hair. Could act white one second, partying like a rock star with the white folks and could act hood the next second, showing off his rims to the thug niggas and they bitches .

His swag was always on fleek, tattoos all over his body and at the time he still had one of his ex's name tatted over his heart; I should've known he was a hoe right then and there. But hell, my momma liked him, my older sister and brother in law loved him; it was almost impossible not to like his ass.

He had me fooled for the longest, he changed over a course of time. He would make me out to be a hoe, even though I wasn't fucking on nobody but him, he had niggas keeping they eyes on me, following me around and shit. I couldn't even buy a CD from a nigga at the gas station without the nigga selling the CD running back trying to tell some shit. Everybody fucked with Chris, and I should've known when he stopped giving a fuck about my feelings something was up.

The nigga would spend days at my house, bring all his clothes and shoes hell even TV just so he could play his game. Then out of nowhere it damn near stopped, I barely saw him, calls and text messages were being ignore, he flipped on me. The nigga started to mind fuck me, it seemed like, if I had a lock on my phone I was a hoe with secrets when the whole time it was actually him keeping the secrets. I shook my head at the thought of it all.

Long story short Chris and I fell all the way off when bitches started posting pictures with him on Facebook wearing matching outfits, and when bitches got brave enough to come to me about a nigga that's supposed to be mine. All that meant was that he made them hoes that comfortable. The nigga played it off though, made it seem like the picture was old and that he didn't know the other bitch. Turned out the picture was taken on Christmas day that year, and this nigga went all out for this bitch with no fucking eyebrows buying her speakers and all sorts of shit and you know what I got? Shit I don't even remember because it was that much of fucking nothing! The bitch didn't even have no eyebrows was my point and no I couldn't fucking get over it, that shit wasn't cute! If you gone fuck off make sure the bitch at least got some damn eyebrows!

I done whooped a bitch ass behind this nigga having hoes come at me sideways, really talking out the side of they necks. So, I whooped the bitch in her baby daddy granny house, I gave no fucks, I didn't take disrespect lightly. Yes, I make house calls, hospital calls and funeral calls, gon show up to that motherfucker like 'bitch I bet you won't die when it's time to die'. I laughed hard at the thought but hell I was serious as a heart attack.

Nevertheless, my ass was still foolish, got back with him after a couple of months and this nigga gone have the nerve to say he done heard this and done heard that knowing his ass ain't heard shit because I stayed to my damn self! But you couldn't tell a nigga that's doing wrong nothing cause you always gone be doing something in they eyes, when they were really doing all the dirt. He didn't care though, he felt like I done been letting the whole city fuck which was his excuse to start using condoms.

My ass was in utter disbelief and chalked it up to that nigga having a guilty ass conscience, later on I found out he was still fucking with that bitch with no damn eyebrows! Pumping that girl head up talking about marriage and shit. He got caught up that time because I called him and the bitch answered the phone.

"Where Chris at?" I asked.

The bitch said, "He in the shower."

"Let me speak with my man since clearly you over there chilling, I'm sure you comfortable enough to walk in the bathroom and give him the phone it ain't like you ain't seen his dick before, shit you there so it must be for the D "

The bitch gone have the nerve to dryly say no then hang up in my face. I was already on the road close to his damn momma house, where the nigga been staying at, the phone call pushed me all the way to my limit. Even though I had my gay best friends and their home girl in the car with me at the time I didn't give two fucks; my mind was gone and all my eyes saw was red.

When I pulled up to the house I seen the bitch ugly ass car parked in front of his house and his car on the side of the house. I got out and knocked on every window and every door but there was no answer. So my ass got in the car that I left parked in the middle of the road and all I could hear was,

"What you doing friend?"

"Don't do it friend, let's just go."

I took the key out of the ignition and dug it all around the sides of his car and then walked to both side mirrors and with one punch them automatic mirrors was out of there. BAM! The nigga had to tie a shoe string around one of them and use a piece of cardboard to hold them up. Needless to say, we stopped fucking with each other for a while, it made me grow a cold heart, any nigga I came across wasn't shit from then on out. I started treating niggas like the dogs that they were so much to the point that I got labeled as a player.

Call it what you want, I wasn't gone let no nigga rip away these walls down again; not ever and I mean ever again in life! I had a soft spot for Chris though, even though I tried to act hard in his presences, I wasn't able to deny the nigga pussy, I still let him fuck because in all honesty he was all I ever wanted. I could never figure out what I did so wrong to deserve to be treated like a nobody; like nothing at all. The dog in him would never die, he always thought every bitch was out to get him, and like I always told him if you weren't doing the hoe ass shit you was doing bitches wouldn't keep fucking with his car. I wasn't the first nor the last bitch to fuck his ride up, he just didn't learn. Females fucked with a nigga's car because they knew that's all they cared about. Even though I never did it again, he had his way of getting many thots in they feelings behind him. The thing that cut me the deepest is when he finally came out and told me that he had been fucking with one of my friends, he told me to watch out but would never tell me who. That was the last straw for me and Chris. Thinking about all the shit really made me sick to my stomach. Still to this day, I never knew what friend he was talking about, he only said that she had evil ways and to watch who I had around me. It was nothing but an emotional roller coaster, I was too over the shit!

I closed my eyes and laid down, as soon as I got comfortable enough to finally go to sleep my phone started going off left and right, like what the fuck I wish motherfuckers would just leave me the fuck alone but that seemed like too much to ask for! Rolling over on my side I grabbed my phone looking at the screen. There was several messages from Trixie, I was about to put my phone down but something inside of me told me to go ahead and read the messages. I instantly got confused and had to reread them!

'I really need to talk to you.'

The next one read.

'It's really important girl'

The third one said,

'I know what really happened to you delete this message after you read this somebody is watching me'

Rolling my eyes, I knew she couldn't possibly know what happened unless she was the one fucking with me the whole time. A gut wrenching, feeling told me that she most likely didn't have nothing to do with it whatsoever. I decided to call her ass back and there was no answer, but a text saying,

'Set up a p.o box so I can mail you some information there. Your house aint a safe place. I cant send it to you there. If you ain't ever trusted me before bitch please trust me now, too many eyes and ears around for me to tell you in person real nigga shit, there is some foul shit going on girl that's all I can say right now.'

I didn't know what else to say besides okay because of the simple fact that Trixie ain't never sounded so serious about anything.

Even though it was via text she never came at me like that about anything, even when the shit was going on between her and Kodak, she never shed any light on the situation. I was sure she was glad that I never decided to bust her out about it; it wasn't my place or my business. It was a bitch named karma that always came back around to bite her dumb ass. Feeling unsure, I had a strange urge to find out about whatever she was talking about; it was going to bug the fuck out of me.

****

The next morning, I rolled over looking at the time and immediately had Trixie all on my brain so I tried to call her again, but there was no answer and she didn't bother to text either. I decided to go ahead and set up a p.o box, I changed into something more comfortable and left out the house heading south towards the post office. It was busy as fuck when I pulled into the parking lot, I almost thought about turning around, but something inside was yelling for me to stay and get to the bottom of it maybe Trixie did know something I didn't know about.

I was feeling real dumbfounded here lately and this bitch was leading me to believe that she knew more about what was going on in my life than I did at the moment. How could that be possible, *'Hell I won't know unless I find out'*, I told myself as I was getting out of the car, it took me about 30 minutes before I got to the front of the line. The lady gave me 2 small keys for my p.o box and I was on my way out the door with my phone in my hand, when I got in the car I sat there for a few seconds before I decided to text Trixie.

'you bet not be bull shiting I just spent money getting this damn po box. If the shit you got to say nothing, then I'm going to beat yo ass for trying to play me like a fool that you think that I am I done already been through enough these last

few weeks here, go the address po box. 3 Houston, Texas. 77001 send what you go and send as soon as possible.'

She texted back damn near immediately saying,

'Usually I'd hehe and haha with you but this shit ain't no joke! you think shit funny now but you'll see something aint right! I don't have all the evidence right now, but I got some shit that will peak your interest, I need you to trust me regardless of what you think about me right now, when she hit the fan, you'll know for show that everything ain't right or what it seem like girl, I advise you not to tell anybody what I'm telling you, these motherfuckers is crazy outchea I'm trying to find out more before a motherfucka I realize I'm snooping, I'll send some more paperwork.'

Rereading the message, I debated on whether to snap or not, because I really was starting to feel like this bitch didn't know shit by the way shit was sounding, but I went ahead and decided to give her the benefit of the doubt and texted her back,

'I'll be waiting bitch.'

All I knew ws that this bitch had better not been up to no foogazy ass shit because she couldn't be trusted; she was dirty, always trying to come up off the next motherfucker! Disregarding what Trixie said about not talking to anyone about it I called Tesea to talk about what was going on. With all this crazy bullshit going on in my life I needed to talk to someone familiar' someone I knew had my back no matter what. Who better than my best friend? I let her know that I needed her to come over as soon as possible.

I wasn't going to mention anything about Troy, I just couldn't bring myself to break her heart or lose my best friend. I knew if I told her our friendship would never be the same; if we even had one after the bullshit.

In an hour while waiting, I cleaned the house a little which wasn't much because I stayed by myself and was hardly ever home. Honestly, this was the most I had ever stayed at home like that, usually I was at the club on nights like this but with the shit going on, I've been cutting back on my hours; I hadn't been feeling going to work, How the fuck could I? I wanted to know a bitch that could! I seriously doubted anyone could take this many blows and still be able to focus on everyday life, if any bitch could deal with the nonsense and still maintain her sanity, I'd applaud her, because I seriously doubted another bitch could.

*****

I opened the door so fast when Tesea rang the doorbell almost knocking my bestie over, embracing her in a huge ass hug, I pulled her inside with a huge sigh of relief.

"Bitch what's gotten into you?" she said inbetween laughs

"Bitch you just don't know! Did you see that damn video of me and Kodak before that shit got shut down ? "

She stopped laughing, almost too quickly, but I didn't think anything about it.

"Yeah bitch, I seen it! Yo mama would shit a brick if she ever got wind of that shit!" she said as we walked into the kitchen. I grabbed a bowl of chocolate covered strawberries and 2 bottles of water before heading back to the living room.

"Girl I know, that's why I'm so glad the shit got taken down! I don't even know who the fuck posted it; girl shits been crazy these last couple of weeks!"

Shaking her head at me she said, "Damn bitch you gave it up to that nigga real quick! I thought you all just started talking, now yo ass all over social media making a name for yourself."

Drinking some of the water out of my bottle I said, "Girl I never planned on giving the nigga the time of day, there was just something about his ass, but I will say a lot of crazy ass shit has been happening and going on since I started talking to him."

Tesea started shaking her head again before saying, "I told yo ass that nigga ain't the nigga you should be fuckin with, he not the one for you!"

"Bitch that ain't what you said!" I said laughing a little too hard apparently because Tesea clearly didn't think it was too funny

"He made you look like a hoe."

Surprised as fuck at what she said I almost spit my water out my mouth. "Girl how the hell he make me look like a hoe when he ain't the one that posted the shit or taped it?" she wasn't moved by my statement.

"Look girl, I just don't want you to get hurt by no buster ass nigga. I'm just thinking about the real world and how it goes, I don't want him dragging your name through the mud; the motherfuckers already think the worst of strippers like you. I'm just looking out for your best interest girl, leave that nigga alone! Ain't no telling who all on his dick in the industry he in."

Tesea felt so strongly about the situation and I wasn't going to argue with her about it; we changed the subject and talked for about an hour before she left .

Chapter 9

The next morning was Friday and the conversation with Tesea was replaying in my mind. Why was she so passionate about what was going on in my life? She was almost too passionate. I figured I was reading way too much into what she for said. With all that was going on I was thinking too deeply because I knew she was a good, down ass friend that was just looking out for me. I got out of bed and started my daily routine, after I finished getting dressed I checked my phone. It was already 10:30 am, so I headed to the post office to check the p.o box. Once there, I texted Trixie, to let her know that I made it there and then headed.

My heart started pounding thinking about what could be inside the box. Did Trixie really know something or was she just being extra? I had a strong feeling that whatever it was, would change shit for me in a major way. I took a deep breath and built up the courage to look inside, opening the box I couldn't believe my eyes! It was paperwork stating that Troy was Tesea's adopted brother; now I had really seen it all. Or so I thought..

I dropped the paper not being able to believe my eyes. That shit couldn't be right, my eyes had to be deceiving me; I picked the paper back up and reread it just for confirmation. The shit had to be legit, but I just couldn't bring myself to believe it. I would've thought that Tesea would tell me some shit like this, I thought we told each other everything but apparently not. Maybe she didn't want nobody to know some shit like that because the shit was nasty in its own way. Too damn close to home; it would've never crossed my mind.

Thinking back on the years of our friendship, Tesea really didn't tell me much of anything on her end. It was always the other way around and she'd just listen; I thought that's what made us click. Suddenly I realized as many times as I'd been around Teasea and Troy together I'd never seen them kiss let alone hold hands. Shit I was just thinking my bitch was a little private with her romance due to me never really meeting any of her previous niggas. I thought that maybe this nigga was different, one she found more serious, serious enough to introduce to the world. Finding all this out had me wondering why the fuck she would introduce this nigga, knowing that possibly one day she'd be at risk of somebody finding out.

This shit was gone rack my damn brain! I remembered that Teasea had told me herself that she didn't have any family left, what the fuck was that about? When I met her, she was already independent living on her own at a young age. She once told me that both of her parents had died a few years before she turned eighteen. All she ever said about it was that it was a horrible tragedy, a series of unfortunate events. At the time I didn't want to push her I knew that must've been hard losing both parents; me personally I wouldn't want to talk about it either. I figured that one day she'd come around to telling me, but that day never came, and I never asked not wanting to open up old wounds.

Now I was more curious than ever, wanting to know what actually happened to her during those years that her parents were alive. Maybe she wanted Troy around to feel a little bit closer to having a family again; as fucked up as that sounds. But Troy just popped up out of the blue not to long ago. She never even told me how they met, all I knew is that at the time I was just happy for my bitch. Happy that she had found happiness, I never questioned her love for the nigga, or said anything bad to her about him.

Shit she knew we didn't get along, I just never knew what the hell he had against me to always be acting so slick nasty towards me. The only night he was somewhat nice to me was the night the nigga raped me. I knew deep down in my soul that he had did it; Trixie even said herself that she left with ol girl and the other niggas. But then again how did I know if all that was true or not, how the hell do I really know what happened that night, or that Trixie really had nothing to do with it. Shit she might've, I couldn't quite put my finger on it but something wasn't right. Why the fuck would go through all that damn trouble, but stay the fuck in my face? Unless Trixie was mad about me fucking with Kodak. Dick aint that damn serious to be acting like that though! Why go through all the chaos if she was the one doing all the fuck shit going on. Shit was making less and less sense to me and it dawned on me that I needed to talk to Trixie face to face; even if I had to pull her hoe ass from that damn apartment by her head. I was tired of motherfuckers playing games with me, they were fucking with my mind not to mention   my   money.

****

This was the fifth time that I called Trixie with no answer, I knew her ass wasn't at the club because I already called Big Boy to see if she was up there and he told me flat out that she ain't been coming in. That didn't even sound like her, for her to be missing some money; shit just didn't sit right with me.

My sixth time trying to call her she picked up on the very last ring, whispering, for God knows what, I was instantly irritated.

"Bitch what the fuck are you whispering for, you fucking or something to where you can't answer the phone, bitch I know you been seeing me call you!" I said yelling into the receiver, I was tired of her ass and this bitch still decided to go on whispering, like fuck what I said.

"No girl, it ain't like that, I told you motherfuckers watching me."

The bitch said it so low I could barely hear her ass.

"Well I got what you sent me in the mail nigga, I don't really make it out to be true, but we need to talk in person, all this secrecy shit making my damn head hurt"

" I can't, I don't want nobody following me!" she was still whispering.

"Bitch snap out if it, I don't see why you so damn paranoid aint nobody stunting ya monkey ass you tripping Gee straight up! If you that damn worried about it I'll pick you up from the bus station and we can go outside of town and talk in the corner or some shit, imma be over within the hour so be ready!" I hung up and headed out.

******

Trixie was already standing outside behind a damn tree looking fucking crazy by the time I made it to the bus station. This bitch had done lost her ever loving mind, knowing good and damned well them hips of hers wasn't gone fit behind no fucking tree. Laughing out loud I blew the horn; this bitch was taking whatever the fuck was going on way too damn seriously. I ain't ever seen her act like this, even though I never ever chilled with her outside the club, I've only seen the hoe around like everybody else.

Reaching over the passenger seat. I opened the door for Trixie as she was running from behind the tree. I noticed that this bitch was wearing all black with her turtle neck covering her mouth, some black combat boots and some dark ass sunglasses like we was about to go rob some motherfuckers. I almost busted out laughing again because this fool looked fucking ridiculous and was doing too much. Once she was inside the car she said nothing and slid all the way down in the seat fastening her seat beat, I drove off shaking my head. After we were out of the parking lot, I spoke first,

"Girl why the fuck is you dressed like that?" she didn't say anything, she was just looking over her seat trying to look out the back side windows. This hoe was going crazier than I was, I could see it through the shades, but I couldn't understand why. Or what the fuck or who the fuck had gotten in to her. Hopefully once we reached one of the towns on the outskirts, she would stop acting so damn crazy! About an hour later we were pulling into Corpus Christie, I drove to one of the beaches downtown that had RV parks nearby, I parked my car in a RV park called *Sunshine,* and turned off the car.

"Now I doubt anybody would follow ya ass all the way down here, so take that damn turtle neck from off ya face!"

Hesitating, she pulled the turtle neck from over her mouth. I got out of the car and waited for her to get out as well so we could walk towards the beach. Trixie's ass finally got out the car about two minutes later, her ass was tripping, I didn't know whether to take her seriously or with a grain of salt. We walked to the beach close to the waters; it was beyond beautiful.

Trixie finally decided to open her mouth once we got down by the water saying,

"We really should keep walking, up and down the beach I mean." She still was whispering sounding like somebody's baby.

"What the hell are you still whispering for? There is nobody else around girl, look to see for yourself! "

Starting to walk, I could see out the corner of my eye that this bitch was really looking around to see. When we got further along the beach I couldn't hold my patience anymore, we were defeating the purpose of coming.

"So what the fuck do you know Trixie? We didn't come out here for no romantic moon light walk! What the hell got you all paranoid and jumpy, tell me what the fuck is really going on!" she looked both ways before opening her mouth .

"I can't tell you much, because I don't know everything right now," she paused then continued on, "I heard Troy on the phone before me and the others left that night, I didn't get to hear who it was because I was too busy trying to play it off like I wasn't ear hustling, nevertheless, Troy ass was on the phone with somebody it sounded like a female and I personally felt like it was Tesea. I wouldn't've really paid too much attention to it if he wasn't trying to be all extra sneaky at his own bachelor party. He told her that everything was still on track and that everybody was leaving except you which made me double look at you slumped over, as soon as I looked up Troy was looking me dead in the eyes, telling the female on the phone that he would handle anything that got out of hand."

"So. if that's true, why didn't you stay with me if you knew something was seeming a little funny?" I side-eyed her as she looked around again.

"Because, the nigga had a gun in his hand and told me to get to stepping, so I rushed behind the others, forgetting my phone inside, I ran back in real quick to see you already on the bed with the door wide open with the gun going in and out of ya pussy. I almost passed out but grabbed my phone and ran out as soon as he looked up and saw me he paused some type of camcorder. Ever since then I've felt eyes and ears everywhere, somebody's been following me, before you even speak that's why I started to do some digging of my own because something ain't right about them. I don't give a damn what you say, bitch I know what I'm talking about and them motherfuckers are crazy. I think they killed they parents, I was waiting to talk to one of Tesea's old friends from her childhood, I know that's ya best friend and all but did the bitch ever tell you both of her parents were murdered in cold blood." This bitch didn't stop for one second to take a breath.

"Whoa, whoa, woah, where the fuck are you getting all this shit from, you don't even know Tesea or her family! Out of all the hoe ass shit you've said or done, that was the lowest thing you could ever say about a motherfucker that you don't even conversate with, like were the fuck do you get off Trixie, damn, the fuck has gotten into you, have you finally lost it for real? "

All the shit sounded so crazy that I really couldn't bring myself to believe anything this bitch was talking about. How the hell you gone try to say my best friend probably murdered her own folks? What the fuck did she know, clearly nothing or she would've came straight forward with some real evidence. This bitch didn't have shit but her mouth and how the fuck was I supposed to be able to trust in a liar, let alone somebody I don't even fuck with? Trixie had me 38 hot but she stood calmly beside me like she was waiting on me to chill out.

"You don't have to believe me, all I can tell you is what I already told you, you can check the internet you know the world wide web like I did and see the shit about her folks nigga! It's not like it was a secret, it was news worthy, I don't have a reason to lie, all I know is I'm going to find out the truth! Whether you like it or believe it, you need to stop being so damn naive and watch your surroundings and the motherfuckers that's your so called best friends! I'm going to send you something to your P.O Box to show you how deep the shit really runs, but you hardheaded nobody can tell you nothing without you ready to pounce. I need to get out of the open, can you please take me home now?"

She really went in on me on the cool, I didn't even say nothing back just headed back to the car to take her ass home.

Chapter 10

I was so glad for Trixie's ass to be out of my car, I headed towards the house, this was too much shit to take in at one time. Shit sounded so fucked up, who could possibly believe all that shit? I knew my friend and I was deciding to give her the benefit of the doubt, I figured there was no way she could pull some hoe shit like that; not on me anyway. That was my pooh bear, the bitch ain't ever acted crazy around me. No matter what she never showed a temper, never lost her cool; that was the thing I loved most about her. She was always the voice of reason, and was always there when needed. How could I believe that shit, she was my down bitch. On the other hand Trixie said she seen the shit with her own eyes, which wasn't saying much at all; I could never trust her. I heard what she had to say but I was choosing my friend over some trick. Once inside the house I threw my purse on the couch and headed for the shower. I could hear my phone ringing with a text message to follow, I was in no rush to get it; my brain had reached its capacity for the day. Standing in the shower, I began to think about Kodak and why he hadn't hit me up.

I thought maybe Trixie was just trying to get close to me to get closer to Kodak, only thing wrong with that thought was that she never once mentioned anything about Kodak so that couldn't be it. Pushing everything to the back of my head I rinsed my body off and got out the shower and grabbed my towel to dry off. I didn't bother putting on my robe, fuck it, wasn't nobody in here. Walking out into the open space of my bedroom, I plopped on the bed butt ass naked, I was physically and emotionally tired. Deciding whether or not to check my phone, I laid there for a few more minutes before reaching my arm lazily over the opposite side of the bed and seen that I had a text from Kodak; guess I thought his ass up. I couldn't help but to smile at the screen though, I missed him but I hated to admit the shit, and I definitely didn't want him to know the shit. Rereading his text, it said,

'You been missing in action ma, get at me.'

Realizing he sent the text 30 minutes ago, I quickly replied,

'I've been getting money where the fuck you been lol.'

He didn't reply back right away so I laid back and watched the ceiling before rolling out of bed to put on my polka dotted booty shorts and hot pink tank top with my pink fuzzy slippers. I grabbed my Mac book heading towards the dining room table. Going towards the fridge, I opened it, grabbed a water bottle and sat down so I could open up my Mac book. First thing I did was go to Pandora to listen to something to get my mind off all of the bullshit.

August Alsina's song. *Let Me Hit That*, blasted through my tiny speakers, I couldn't help but to sing along to it that was my shit.

"Super loud , super strong , super green got me super gone, that super oooo, that super high , like super man cuz I'm super fly."

I was singing along hitting every note, I loved that sexy ass nigga; good God was he fine. I almost didn't hear my phone go off cause I was singing so loud. Looking at the phone screen Kodak had finally texted back and said he was on his way to me. This nigga just loved popping up, I was glad though, because really I was starting to get lonely and I actually missed his company and attention and even his big ass ego. There was just something about him I couldn't shake.

******

Before I knew it, Kodak was at the door, looking fine as always but mad as ever. He didn't even give me a chance to speak before he start getting on my head.

"Who the fuck ya ass been talking to my nigga? When I tell you that you need to watch who the fuck you around that's what the fuck I mean ya Digg? Don't play stupid either Kayla cause I ain't about to play with ya ass."

He looked like he wanted to slap me dead across my face, that's all I could think about as he kept talking,

"Don't play with me, play with them niggas, my patience running real fucking thin. You think a nigga like me ain't gone know. You think a nigga like me ain't gone get told by the next motherfucker?"

Stepping aside I let his ass in, he was bugging straight tripping and I really didn't know what the fuck he was talking about

"Nigga, I don't know why you handling me like that cause I really don't know what yo ass talking bout, you talking out the side of ya neck right now. Chill out my dude."

He looked at me like he was about to slap the spit out my mouth,

"Nah ya ass need to chill the fuck out, while you out here acting foolish, I'm gone tell you one more time watch who the fuck you have around you cause if something happen to ya real hard headed ass imma have to murk a nigga, real shit."

"Tell me what the fuck you talking about, for real cause I really have no idea, why you coming at me like that in my house? Shit, I thought you wanted to see me but you came over here to bitch me out about nothing!"

He was still looking at me like he could just slap my ass and I noticed he didn't have his double cup today.

"Say watch ya mouth shawty, I did come over here to see ya ass, I just got to let it be known though, shit ain't what it look like, stop running ya mouth to motherfuckers."

I sat down on the arm of the couch with my hands clasped together.

"I really don't know what you talking about; I been at the house chilling." I rolled my eyes

"Yeah you know, you just think I don't, I'm just looking out for ya shawty I ain't trying to see you get hurt out herr. Big boy told me you ain't been coming to work on the regular like you supposed to, I ain't even too much trying to have you dance for my niggas no more, what's between them thighs is mine. Shit you can feature in a few videos or whatever but as for stripping, I ain't too much feeling that shit no mo, not for you anyway. I'd rather ya nose be in a book, it ain't too late to go back to school, you don't have to strip to prove you independent ma, niggas know."

Kodak walked to me and lifted my legs from underneath me making me land on my back on the couch, within seconds he was on top of me making me forget what the hell he was even talking about, breathing in my face looking me in my eyes.

"You really must not know all your worth ma, you too beautiful for this shit, too smart even with ya fly ass mouth."

He started kissing on my neck all the way down to my inner thighs, he slid my shorts aside and kissed the front of my pussy lips, I could feel his dick growing on my leg. He moved my shorts back in place and got up, I almost had a heart attack right then and there.

"That's mine ma, but I don't want you thinking that's all I want from ya."

This nigga wasn't nothing but a tease, what he said was so sweet that my heart started racing even more.

I couldn't allow myself to fall though, I'd been through too much and I refused to go back down that road; how could I be with a nigga that already had it all? What could I really do for him that hasn't already been done? Therefore, I couldn't tell if he was spitting game or keeping it real mo matter what he said.

Maybe I was just too stubborn or maybe I had built these walls around my heart too high. I knew that if I could barely take Chris and his side hoes then I really wouldn't be able to take Kodak and his fans. He must of knew I was deep in thought because he just stood there looking down at me for the longest without saying anything. After a few moments he finally spoke up,

"Look ma, I already know you been fucking on another nigga, shit I ain't mad at you. You ain't ready for the shit yet, but from here on out you bet not spread them legs for no nigga or I'm gon knock ya ass out."

I looked at him like he was crazy as hell, I hadn't fucked on nobody.

"What you talking about Kodak?"

"Don't play stupid"

He pulled out his phone and showed me a thirty second video clip of Troy fucking me from the back, even though all you could see was pussy and dick slapping together; I knew it was him.

Chapter 11

Suddenly I couldn't breathe, shit was still getting flipped upside down, how was I supposed to maintain with shit going the way it was going. Realizing I was gasping for air Kodak placed his hands on my shoulders.

"Breathe ma"

Trying to slow my breathing, I put my hand over my chest.

"Where did you get that from?" My voice was shaky.

"Never mind all that, I ain't mad at ya shawty."

That alone just let me know that he had no idea what really happened. The video was just another piece to a bigger picture, I was utterly disgusted, another thirty second clip that didn't show really anything. Whoever taped it made sure they didn't identify who it was that was raping me. Just by going off the video Kodak received, it didn't look like rape at all, it just looked like I was taking the dick .

"Just tell me who sent that, because its not what it looks like I can promise you that."

"To be real, I don't even know my damn self, it was sent to me out of the woodworks after I called you earlier. I ain't tripping though ma, the shit dead, it's already a done deal. Just remember what I said, don't let the shit happen again or imma have to beat ya ass ya dig, ain't nobody playing with you Kay."

This nigga wasn't even my nigga but at that moment he made it very clear that he was. I wasn't going to argue with him and I didn't have the strength in my body to tell his ass what really happened that night. What good would it really do when I wasn't too sure myself, I was just gone let the shit ride for now. Not knowing what else to sat to him I just bawled up on the couch and stayed there until he said he had to go. He lifted my chin with his index finger and told me he'd see me soon. All I could do was sit there and nod. It wasn't until he went out the door that it dawned on me that Trixie might know what she was talking about. I just didn't want to feed into it, but shit was getting out of hand. I made up my mind that I was going to give Trixie the benefit of the doubt as well. Why go through all the trouble if there wasn't some kind of truth to what she was saying?

******

Showing up for work a few days after my visit from Kodak, I wasn't feeling it. Apparently Big Boy could tell and had me just work the floor instead of performing that night. I took niggas drink orders and gave a few niggas a lap dance.

After only two hours I was about ready to bounce until I seen out the corner of my eye that Troy homeboys from that night were sitting in the VIP section watching me like a hawk.

Crazy thing was that I had never seen them niggas in the club before, so what the fuck was they really doing here now? Maybe I was just paranoid, or it was all in my head. Trying to make sure it was one or the other or both I turned my head in their direction to make sure I wasn't seeing shit. My eyes looked straight at the VIP section and sure enough it was both of the niggas from that night. Once they noticed me looking their way they smiled and motioned for me to come over. Second guessing myself, I pushed myself in their direction, something didn't seem right about their presence being in the club. Walking up to the table one of the niggas could see the look of annoyance written all over my face,

"Ya G string must be too tight shawty, that's why ya face frowned up huh shawty?" he laughed at his own smart ass comment.

"First of all nigga, I ain't ya shawty, second of all what's two bum ass niggas like you doing here? I know y'all ain't got no money so what do you need?" They both looked at each other and laughed then looked at me suddenly turning serious. Rolling my eyes I said, "You got something to say nigga then say it, hell!"

"You got a fly ass mouth, lil momma ain't nobody stunting you, we here looking for Trixie."

Taken aback a little, I waited a moment before speaking again,

"What the hell you want with Trixie? She not here and I'm sure she don't want nothing to do with y'all asses."

The other ugly motherfucker started to stand and up but the other one that was still sitting down motioned to his partner to sit down as well.

"Watch ya mouth, as for all the other shit you talking about, it ain't ya damn business lil bitch."

I could've spit on his ass, but I didn't. Not knowing what else to do I just walked away, I could feel their eyes burning in the back of my neck; I didn't like the feeling. I knew I wasn't going to be able to get anything out of they ass anyway so I really don't know why the fuck I went over there anyway. Deciding I really didn't want to be in the club anymore, I headed to the back and grabbed my shit to leave.

On my way out the door I felt a sharp tug on my hair, I tried to spin around but my face was instantly slammed against the side if the door frame. Hot breath was blowing on the back of my neck, and then the voice from one of Troy's niggas was seeping into my ear and his funky ass breath was burning the inside of my nose.

"You ain't so tough now huh, thinking you the baddest bitch in these streets."

He shoved my face harder into the door frame as I tried to wiggle free from his grip.

"You move when I say you can hoe, now listen to me very carefully cause I'm only gone say this once, keep ya nose on ya face and not out of place and when you do see Trixie tell her I got somebody that want to see her."

He pulled my head away from the door frame and slapped my ass so hard it felt like my left cheek was about to fall off. He walked out the room laughing like nothing had ever happened. Shocked at what just happened, I rubbed the back of my head to find it throbbing, rushing out the door I didn't even bother to look back or even tell anyone   I   was   leaving.

******

Not knowing where to go, I just sat in my car trying to take deep breaths in order to calm myself down. Finally turning the car on, I looked behind me before putting it in reverse. I could hear my phone getting a text alert, I waited until I pulled out completely before putting my foot on the break to check my phone. I had a text from Tesea, she didn't ever text me late so I figured something must've been wrong, but to my surprise she said,

'Why you leave the club girl, me and Troy was just coming in'

Damn how the hell did she know I left? I know for a fact I didn't see her or Troy anywhere coming out of the club.

She would've had to ask Big Boy and he didn't mingle like that so that was out, choosing not to respond I took my foot off the break and drove to the end of the parking lot, a rock came flying through my damn window. My breathing started to pick up again and I was thanking the man upstairs that the big ass rock didn't hit me. Speeding off I refused to look back not caring about the speed limit I was ready to get a ticket today. I didn't stop the car until I got all the way to the house. Reaching into the backseat I grabbed the rock that was thrown through the window shield, it had a message taped to it, with the words, 'Be careful ha-ha', written in black sharpie.

Getting out of the car I threw the rock in the street and analyzed my back window. First glance it didn't look that bad, but this was the second time I would have to get my window fixed. I had only made a little less than a stack because I didn't stay the whole shift, on top of that I was on the floor all night instead of performing the way I usually did. Most of the money I made tonight was going to have to go towards my back window.

"Fuck my life man!" I said out loud to myself still standing outside looking at the mess.

Frustration was taking over my body, I just wanted to hit everything in sight!I wanted to forget about it all and for things to go back the way they use to be. Instead of hitting anything I let the tears well over and burn my eyes. I was so tired of the bullshit and fuckery going on, not knowing what I did to deserve it all was a real fucked up feeling. Wiping at my face, I turned around making the decision that I was going to get to the bottom of everything my damn self. I was determined to come out of this shit stronger than I was before, then again that was better said than done. Turning around after looking at the back window for God knows how long, I headed inside the house ready to   throw   it   all   away.

Once I was inside the house I heard a beeping noise that stopped me dead in my tracks right there in the doorway. I flipped on the lights to look around when I noticed cameras in every corner of my living room with a red light that beeped every time it flashed. Running towards every camera I knocked them all down and threw them in the middle of the floor wondering how the fuck somebody got into my house while I wasn't there.

I ran all over the house checking to see if I left a window unlocked. None were open and were all locked just the way I've always left them; I checked the back door but there was no sign of forced entry. Now I was more confused and scared as ever, I couldn't figure out how somebody could have gotten inside. Going back over to the four cameras I was curious to know who was watching on the other end. Without thinking twice about it, I stomped every last one of them motherfuckers and left all the pieces in the middle of the floor.

Now more than ever I thought about Trixie and everything she said. Telling me how she had been feeling like she was being followed, more and more it started to sound like there was some truth to what she was saying which made my skin crawl. I grabbed my phone and start trying to call her, she didn't answer, I tried again and she still didn't answer, my foot was tapping uncontrollably waiting to see if she would eventually pick up the phone but I wasn't to sure if she would cause of the way she'd been acting lately. After ten more try's I gave up on calling and decided to text her that I needed to talk to her.

Two hours later she still hadn't responded which wasn't like her, but I figured she might be too paranoid to answer any calls so I decided to just drive to her apartment and pop up on her. I wasn't about to second guess myself, so I grabbed my keys as fast as I could and headed her way. Once I arrived at her apartment complex I got this strange feeling before I decided to park and go upstairs, it was like the hair on my arms didn't start sticking up until I arrived over there. I walked upstairs to her apartment and once I made it completely up the stairs the door was wide open, but the lights were off.

I walked inside and turned on the lights while calling out her name, but there was no response . I walked over to the kitchen and seen a dingy stretched out condom hanging out the deep freezer. *The fuck kind of freak is this bitch?* I thought to myself, hesitating whether or not to open it. I opened it and found Trixie inside looking beyond lifeless, with different colored condoms around her neck and a bullet hole in between her eyes. I held my hand over my mouth and stepped back trying not to trip over my own feet.

CHAPTER 12

I jumped back so far that I almost landed on top of her coffee table. Trying to hold myself together I eased my way back over to the deep freezer and looked down at Trixie, there were all different colors and sizes of condoms stretched out and tied together in knots to connect to the other one. The condoms were wrapped so tight around her neck that it looked like it was breaking into her skin. The thing that scared me the most was that her mouth and eyes were still wide open. The shit was just unbelievable, I had to get the fuck out of there, but not before I looked around first. The apartment itself was pretty nice, she had a tan sectional with nice marble end tables and a pretty glass coffee table with rhinestones going around the edge of the glass. A 50 inch flat screen TV sat on an oak TV stand with plants hanging from the ceiling on both sides with beautiful African pictures hanging all over the walls.

Nothing seemed out of place in the living room so I walked down the hall and looked in her bedroom, on top of the queen size canopy bed she had two large suit cases. Looking around some more, I noticed that every drawer was empty and every cabinet in the bathroom. *Trixie must've been going somewhere. But where?* I thought to myself.

"Where were you going Trixie?" I whispered out loud.

Then I noticed her laptop on the side of her bed and picked it up thinking that maybe if I looked through the history I could have some sort of idea on where she was headed to. It wasn't safe here, clearly, so I decided to take the laptop with me. I tried to find her phone but I was too scared to keep looking so I rushed out. As soon as I stepped out the door I called the police and reported someone's house getting broke into at the apartments.

I didn't want to involve myself like that, letting it be known that I was inside the apartment all it would do was make matters worse or I'd end up just like Trixie so I had to lay low and not involve anyone else in it for that matter. Shit was really hitting rock bottom. I never thought for one second that anyone would turn up dead, especially not Trixie, unless it came from a STD. Sad to say but it was the truth, she knew she was a hoe. Even she didn't deserve to die; not like that. Whoever did this shit was a foul ass human being, how the fuck you gone kill somebody in they own shit and stuff they damn body in they own damn deep freezer? The shit was crucial; way too much to take   in.

******

Deciding that I didn't want to be at my house alone, I drove to a holiday inn and paid for a room for an entire week. I instantly felt safer once I was inside my room. Sitting at the desk I opened

Trixie's laptop, thankfully it wasn't wiped cleaned when I opened up the internet browser. Clicking on her history for the last thirty days, I found out that she had a plane ticket for San Diego California scheduled to leave at eight thirty tomorrow morning.

Shaking my head, I went to her Gmail; she was still logged into. Scrolling through her emails I found that there were ten starred ones. I noticed that all of them were from a female named Liah Dansby. Looking over the name I remembered Teasea told me she used to have a best friend with the last name Dansby. She told me that when we had first met each other because she said I reminded her of her. Looking over the email it said,

'I'll be waiting at the airport with a sign near the entrance, you won't be able to miss it.'

Exiting out of that email, I went ahead and looked at the next starred one inside was a picture of her, Tesea and Troy. Underneath it said, '*I loved him until his mind became brainwashed*'. The more I read the more disgusted I became. I found her number and saved it in my phone. Figuring it wouldn't be wise to call, I set up my own plane ticket to San Diego, the earliest one I could get was leaving the same time Trixie's was supposed to leave at eight thirty tomorrow morning.

All I needed was my purse and my phone I didn't want to take anything with me when I could just get it on the way or once I touched down in Cali. I was going to look at this like a mini vacation. I needed to get away and be in the sun surrounded by palm trees, but I'm not gon lose sight of why I'm going. There was no turning back now, I was going to finish what Trixie had started but the smart way; whatever that was. I was still not too sure if Tesea really had something to do with it, I needed to know for myself and now for Trixie.

I couldn't sleep, I was too afraid somebody's ass might be lurking somewhere outside the hotel so I stayed up until the morning. When the sun was trying to rise up, I turned off the TV and headed out not feeling safe there anymore.

I was starting to feel paranoid like Trixie was when I had seen her the last time we met. I hated the feeling, but you could never be too careful. Looking both ways when I was on the outside of the room I rushed to the car and headed towards the airport. I didn't bother stopping for gas or to get something to eat real quick. I still had at least an hour before the plane was supposed to take off. I found a parking spot in the airport's parking lot and decided it was the safest place to leave the car.

My legs felt like they couldn't move, and my arms felt the same. I don't know if it was because I was paranoid, but I knew I needed to get myself some act right before I got on this plane. Breathing in deeply I sat there for a couple of more seconds before getting out the car. I locked the door behind me and checked the back window again, I didn't have time to get it fixed. Double looking over the hole in the window, it wasn't big enough for a motherfucker to put nothing through it but their fist. After acknowledging that, I went inside the airport and waited for my plane to arrive.

*****

Boarding the plane I felt more nervous than I ever had, under my breath I kept asking myself what the fuck was I doing. It was too late to turn around, there was no going back, I was already one step closer than I was before. I just hated that I had to go through this shit alone, I couldn't tell Kodak what was going on exactly because I really didn't know too much myself right now and I didn't want to bring anyone else in on my problems.

Honestly a small part of me blamed Kodak for the shit that was going on, I thought he had something to do with the shit, the way he acted though proved differently. Who could I trust though. He told me to trust no one so that's what the hell I was going to have to do and that meant him too. The flight only took hours instead of days, thank God cause I swear I was about to start getting sick. Once we landed, I went to the subway inside the airport just to sit down and book a room online at the Quality Inn. I booked a king size suite so apart of me could feel at home on this trip. Once I had a room booked I had to call a cab and wait forever for it to arrive due to traffic.

Shit was way more hectic down here, I loved the sight of the palm trees though because they seemed so peaceful, everybody looked happy I'm guessing because it was Cali, the place where it usually doesn't rain. It felt good to be here, even though the air was humid as hell and felt like the soles of my shoes would melt into the concrete. The humid air made me sweat and I had to find a clothing store cause I refused to walk around musty, that's that shit I don't like.

Cali was so real though because they had a little boutique inside the airport, I went inside and grabbed just anything, blue jean shorts, tank tops and a couple of pair of different color flip flops. Not realizing by the time I got outside the boutique somebody was grabbing my damn cab like they was the one that called it. Starting to head outside I called the cab company while I sat on the bench outside and waited another forty-five minutes, sweating my ass off while motherfuckers walking by were looking at me crazy. When I finally was inside the cab I had him take me straight to the hotel I was too tired to do anything else.

******

When morning came I was up bright and early ready to head down to meet this girl named Liah, I hoped and prayed this bitch wasn't crazy cause only God knows how much more I could take of this foolishness. I called the cab and waited for it to arrive. Once the cab came it only took twenty-five minutes to arrive outside of Liah's beautiful condo. I was stunned at how good it looked. Not being able to turn around I went ahead and walked up to the door, which was opened immediately before I could even knock on the door. She spoke,

"I was expecting you, Kayla isn't it? Trixie said if she couldn't make it you would, come inside love."

I smiled taken back a little, she didn't even ask how I found out where she stayed at. She led me into her living room and motioned me to sit down.

"It's nice to meet you," I started, "I didn't mean to pop up unannounced, but I figured it was the best way."

She looked at me like she was expecting me to say everything all at once.

"I know why your here Kayla, we can skip right to it, no need for small talk, you came here for answers and I'm not sure I can give you them all, but I can give you some insight. Me and Tesea grew up together since we were babies, when we grew up she started lusting over her father. Me and Troy started dating and he would tell me about it all the time until she started seducing and drugging him, she convinced him to help her sleep with her father and when her father refused she killed both her momma and daddy."

Chapter 13

My eyes were bulging out of my sockets from the information Liah was so forth coming with. Like this bitch didn't sugar coat anything! I was confused as fuck and needed her to clear it   up, but she didn't give me a chance to speak because she was still going on.

"Troy came to me crying, telling me everything and said how him and Tesea had to move away, start a new life and change their last names"

I waited to see if she was going to continue, when she didn't I spoke up,

"I don't mean to be rude, but how the hell would you know if that was true or not? Did you witness everything yourself, Tesea is a very beautiful girl, so I wouldn't see her having a problem with getting any man she wanted. Her trying to fuck on her daddy seems a little much don't you think?"

Liah paced around the living room looking at me dead on the whole time.

"I never said I believed it all, that's just what I was told by Troy. What I do know for sure is that the parents did die inside the house were they use to stay. They lived in the hood, I can promise you the life Tesea lives now is not the life she use to have, on top of all that I don't see why Troy would lie about something like that."

With that being said Liah decided to take me down to were Tesea and Troy use to stay, first she had to grab a few things before we headed out I noticed she had to set a alarm system as well; something that I obviously needed. Setting the code she was ready to go.

******

Downtown was further from her house than I thought and it wasn't the downtown I expected, she literally meant downtown were the hood was at and not the city life. Passing through the hood I seen gangs, bad ass kids running through the streets not looking for cars ain't no telling where they mommas was at. Motherfuckers sitting on porches drinking, playing dice and bootlegging.

Liah pulled up in front of the house that was suppose to be Teasea's when she was a child, it was an old two story house that looked like it didn't belong in the hood. Me and Liah got out the car at the same time and stood on the side walk in front of the fence.

You could tell there use to be a glass door, that was probably once beautiful but now shattered . The windows were gone and the roof had caved in from I guess the fire. Standing right there I could see inside everything was burnt and fallen apart. I wondered why they just haven't torn it down instead of leaving the mess that was once a house; there wasn't much to see now.

"See over there was her parents bedroom." she said pointing to the left window on the opposite side of the house.

"Word around town is that the police was going to rule it as an accidental death, instead they went ahead and did an autopsy and found over seventy acute cuts, they didn't come from broken glass, all over his body that no longer included his balls and dick which were cut off." she shook her head at the thought.

"They never really suspected the kids because they had a solid alibi. They were at their grandmas and grandpa's for the weekend, they stated they never left the house so they were ruled out as suspects, everything about the mom and dad are in the newspapers it was a big thing back then, only thing that isn't in the newspapers is the shit that Troy told me."

Looking away from the house I turned towards her.

"Why didn't you ever tell the police what he told you then?"

Waiting a couple of beats she said,

"Because I loved him, I thought me and him were going to grow old together, until he started to change, I could see it in his eyes that he wanted to stay. Still to this day I don't want nothing to happen to him, I've always kept a place for him in my heart thinking that maybe one day he'd come back to me," she looked up to the sky sighing deeply before carrying on.

"Then somehow your friend Trixie found me, I don't know how, but when she said it had something to do with Tesea, I knew something was up, she didn't feel safe talking on the phone so she planned to come out here. She said if anything happened to her that you would come so I'm guessing something had to happen because you're not the girl I seen in the picture she sent me."

Sighing loudly, I headed back towards Liah's four door Sedan.

"So, you're basically telling me that you waited so long to speak up because you loved Troy and the only reason you're saying something now is because Trixie found out who you are. Shit just still ain't making sense to me, maybe it's just too much to take in, I'll admit a lot of crazy shit has been going on but I just can't bring myself to fully believe that Tesea is capable of doing all this bullshit. She's always been more than nice to me, has been there by my side when shit wasn't going right in my own life. I know she couldn't've possibly committed a crime let alone against me! I know she couldn't've committed a murder, for all I know Troy could have done all this bullshit, and playing you like a dummy because he knows you love him."

Turning around at the car. I noticed that Liah hadn't moved at all, so I spun around to see her eyes in disbelief, without saying anything at all she walked over to the driver side door and paused before opening the car door. Looking at me over the roof of the car she said,

"You're the one that came to me looking for answers so maybe your ass shouldn't be so ignorant and naive! I didn't go looking for you, remember that, so I have no reason to lie!" she stopped for a second and gave a dry laugh and cocked her head back a bit, "What the hell could I possibly get out of that all these years later? Now that's what doesn't make any sense."

She instantly got in the car and didn't say another word, when I tried to open the car door she locked the car and rolled down the passenger window.

"There was no point of coming all this damn way if you were going to be so blind to the truth, you know where to find me when you're ready to listen." And with that she was gone.

*****

I stood there with my mouth wide open in disbelief, this bitch just left me out there, standing on the side of the fucking road looking crazy! I grabbed my phone out my pocket to try to call a cab but I only had one percent.

"Fuck!" I yelled letting the word come out my mouth as loudly as possible.

I forgot to charge my phone last night so I was shit out of luck. I tried to look around to see if there were any friendly faces around that might let me use their phone. First glance there was no one around other than some ratchet ass females up in some nigga's face and a couple of dope boys on the corner.

I decided I was just better off walking the way I came to see if there was a store nearby. As I turned around and started to walk, the front door of Tesea's neighbor's house flung open, I glanced and kept it moving. I wasn't even able to walk past the door all the way before I seen a crippled old lady step out on the porch and started pointing her bony bent finger at me.

"Stop it right there, you evil piece of shit, I know who you are, how dare you come back here after what you've done. Yeah, you might've fooled them white folks but your ass ain't ever been able to pull one over on me."

I stopped in my tracks confused on what the hell this old lady was talking about, pointing her crinkly ass finger at me.

"Ma'am you must have me confused with someone else, this is my first time in life ever coming to Cali!"

Her finger was still in the air pointing dead at me.

"You save that sob story for them folks that give a shit, I've known your spiteful ass since you were a youngin about yay high. Did you really think I wouldn't recognize you little girl, I hope you didn't come back here trying to trick anymore folks into feeling sorry for you. You're going to die alone for all the evil things you've done. I told ya momma to keep your ass on that damn crazy medication since she acted like she didn't know what to do with you anymore. I told her to do it before your true colors started showing, see she didn't want to believe it but I know evil when I see it, you ain't nothing but the devil; a slick ass little girl. I know you killed them. Now you get ya ass outta of here, you don't belong around here, I can smell the evil on you from a mile away." completely stunned I wasn't going to argue with this old lady, clearly, she was not in her right mind.

Me and Teasea looked nothing alike, not to my knowledge anyway. The old lady must didn't have good eyesight. I walked a couple of blocks up the road and stopped at a 7 eleven, the clerk was nice enough to let me use the phone. I called a cab and in the meantime got a warm deli sandwich made. This time it only took the cab twenty minutes to arrive, I had him take me back to the hotel.

*****

Now I was in the hotel room racking my brain with all the information that has been coming towards me today. I started thinking Liah was right and did have a point. I was the one that came all the way down here dropping everything I was doing to find out more about what was going on.

She was right, I was being naive, the old lady had never saw me a day in her life but swore she had and I knew she could only be talking about Tesea. The shit was creeping me the fuck out, I just had a feeling that there were so many more unanswered questions. Then I got to thinking back to what Liah said before she ditched me, 'when you're ready to listen, you know where to find me."

Not thinking twice, I was getting ready to head back to Liah's house. I charged my phone and seen online that they had Uber drivers; I'd never been in one before, but it seemed like it would be faster. Fifteen minutes later, a guy named Dan was dropping me back off at Liahs house. When I stood on the front porch the lights were out in the house and I started getting that feeling again.

I looked at the driveway and noticed the car was right there with Liah inside.

It kind of pissed me off that she obviously seen me standing on the porch looking like a dummy when she was just right there the whole time. I ran over to the car and noticed that her body was slumped over, so I opened the door to find her stabbed in every part of her upper body, it looked like she had twenty stab marks in her breasts alone and had cigarette burns on her eyelids.

Chapter 14

"What the fuck!" I yelled backing away from the car. How could this shit even be fucking possible? I ran up the road as far as I could without stopping. Somebody must've been following me, but how? I made sure that I didn't go straight home. I didn't contact anyone before leaving, I could've sworn I was safe. The only way this could be possible was if somebody was watching my every move. Shit every time I looked around though, there was no one to be found.

I made it five blocks away before I buckled over putting my hands on my knees trying to catch my breath. Looking in all directions I couldn't see anyone in sight, the streets was busy but there wasn't many people walking around this time. Forgetting I even had my phone on me I reached into my back pocket and took it out. Kodak had tried calling a few times, hitting him back up was the last thing on my mind. Not knowing what to do, I called the Uber Driver back to see if he could take me back to the hotel.

I walked to the nearest store so I could meet him there, I didn't want to be on the streets alone. I had to brace myself against the wall of the store in the light while I waited. I was too scared to move anywhere outside of that spot of light and too afraid of what could happen if I moved away from the light. Shit was happening in the blink of an eye and I didn't think I was going to be able to sleep tonight; shit or anytime soon. My eyes were so tired of the tears, I couldn't bring myself to cry now. So, I just stood there impatiently waiting for Dan the Uber Driver while I tried to breathe at a normal pace. Then, after waiting for what felt like forever, he finally arrived.

I wasn't too sure if going back to the room was a good idea, but as of right now I had nowhere else to go. I only got a one-way ticket instead of a round trip ticket so I was stuck for right now and my only hope to getting any answers was dead, like what the fuck? The cigarette burns on Liah's eyelids kept flashing in and out of my mind.

I could tell she had a slow death, the way her and Trixie died was crucial. Even with everything going on and two motherfukers dead I still had a hard time believing it was Tesea; Troy had to have done it. Why wouldn't anyone think he was capable of doing anything, I could see him do it all hell. He was capable of rape, so he damned sure could be capable of murder. That old lady never mentioned anything about Troy though, she said "evil spirited little girl".

I wondered what else she meant. Now it was like I had to backtrack and try to have an open mind. I had to start listening before it was too late and now more than ever I was ready to do that. If that was how I was going to save my life or anybody else's for that matter.

Coming to the conclusion that now the old lady was my hope to learning anything about the past. I just didn't want the old hag to cuss me out like she had done before, and if somebody was really watching me I didn't want to risk whatever life the old lady had left. Because everywhere I've went lately, something beyond fucked up had happened. Shit it looked like that was my only choice though, I refused to leave this place without being able to find out more. Plus, I don't like wasting money, plane tickets ain't fucking cheap.

Before I spend all that money on going back, I was going to get my money's worth while I was here; even if I had to die trying. If I didn't find out what was really going on, my whole life would be ruined. It all just makes me think back to what Kodak said about me going back to school. This shit opened up my eyes making me realize he was right, maybe I need to step down and actually put my brain to use and come up another way. A way that wouldn't eventually kill me.

I wasn't going to be able to enjoy my job after all this shit was over with; if it ever was going to be over with. The only thing I could do was try to fight the shit and get all the facts I possibly could because as of right now, I had absolutely nothing at all but word of mouth. If I would've just listened to Liah she would've never drove off and she would've never died; at least not the way she did. Right now wasn't the time to start blaming myself, if I wanted to get to the bottom of shit I had to first clear my mind, they say if you go looking for something you'll find it and that was exactly what I planned to do.

...

Barely being able to rest, I sat all the way up in the bed and grabbed my phone off the charger. I called the damn Uber man to take me back downtown to see if I could stumble back across this old lady. I didn't want her to shun me when she seen me again so, I decided to look a little more modest not showing any bare skin. Maybe then she could tell the difference between the two of us. Rushing down to the lobby, I sat in one of the lounge chairs close to the front door to watch to see Dan pulling up.

It didn't take him long at all once I had finally got comfortable in the chair. Dan didn't speak much, but he had a bad ass 2016 Nissan Altima. I'd rather be in the car with an Uber driver any day because. A Motherfucker didn't know that you had to pay for the ride. Too bad they didn't have none back home, but with a service like this I'm sure it would spread through all 50 States in the near future. Dan pulled on the street where I had first went with Liah in no time.

The same ratchet females were in niggas faces and the same busted ass dope boys was on the corners. I could never bring myself to stay over here, no matter how bad off I was. Once I seen Tesea's old house I told Dan to pull in front of it. I tossed him his money breathed in and out just a little and got out the car telling Dan to just wait there instead of me calling him back to come all the way across town to get me again.

I was thankful as hell when he said he would wait but only for a minute. I ran up to the old lady's porch and before I could knock the porch lights came on and the door flew open like it had done before, it was like the old lady could sense I was coming, but how? She didn't even give me a chance to speak before she came onto the porch pointing her crusty ass finger in my face wagging it back and forth and coughing up black shit while spitting it out in the grass, the whole time her finger was still moving back and forth in my face.

"What the hell you doing here girl? You got some nerve bringing that evil around me".

"Ma'am I'm sorry to pop up on you, I'm not whoever you think I am, my name is Kayla, my best friend Tesea use to live right next door to you. I just had a few questions".

The old lady slowly started to remove her finger out of my face and looked at me like she didn't believe me then said,

"You got her all over you child, you've been around her so much her presence is on your body or she's somewhere near by".

I looked over my shoulder to see if Dan was still next door and he was so I asked the old lady,

"How long have you been living here ma'am?" she looked at me crazy for a second,

"I've been living here before you was born child and before your evil ass friend was born. That child was always some trouble."

"Why do you keep calling her-"she cut me off mid-sentence.

"Because the little heffa was evil, and I know evil when I see it, let me tell you something about your so-called friend. Them parents of hers were good people, they loved them chillin even the boy that wasn't naturally they own. When the little winch thought nobody else was looking I was. I was always watching, I seen the way she looked at that daddy of hers always sitting on his lap, grinding those nasty hips of hers. You youngins just sicken me, at first, I thought her daddy was touching on her until I noticed he was sleep like a rock. And she would just be on top of him straddling him like a wild animal. I believe she drugged that man, and I believe the mama was scared of her. Because the little skank walked around like she was the mama. Dressing up in her mama's clothes walking around in her shoes all the while she had all the windows open like she liked a show. I seen her put that poison in his mouth and I also seen her put one of them plastic strap things on and rape that mans mouth. So don't tell me she ain't evil."

CHAPTER 15

I tried to speak but the old lady started waving her finger at me.

"I ain't done yet, so don't you speak, I knew that momma of hers was scared of that child because she seen the shit her damn self. I saw her walk in and turn right back around, the shit still makes me sick to my damn stomach. That man did not wake up not one time, it's like his mouth was a damn playground. I don't know what that child gave him but whatever it was knocked him smooth on out. When I heard they were in that fire I knew something wasn't right. I'm the one who called the cops, luckily, they always make it to this area in no time since we in the projects and all. So, when they got there the body's weren't burnt enough for them not to recognize who they were. I know she did it something in my bones told me so and I'm never wrong. You get on out of here now cause that devil all over you, and don't like it. Get I said, and don't you come back here you hear me."

The old lady turned around to go inside and slammed the door in my face. She didn't give me a chance to speak, didn't even let me open my mouth so I just turned around and headed to the car were Dan was waiting.

I was glad he didn't decide to burn out because it seemed like the old ass lady was talking forever. The shit she said was crazy, and I didn't like the fact that she thought Tesea was evil. I just didn't think it was Tesea, how could she be that fast. Somebody was nearby but I didn't think it was Tesea though. Everything in me wanted not to believe Tesea was the person everybody was making her out to be. Just made it seem like I didn't know her that well or not at all. Once I made it to the car I opened the door and sat down without looking over.

"Thank you for waiting, man I didn't even think it would take that long."

Dan didn't speak at all nor did he turn on the car making me decide to look up at him. Dan was holding his stomach, so I looked down to see why he was holding it the way he was. He looked up at me and removed his hand from his stomach to show the blood seeping through his shirt. My instant reaction was to ask him what happened, but he mouthed the word "run."

By that time, it was a little too late, I tried turning around reaching for the door handle trying to open the door as fast as I could but was topped when my hair was grabbed so hard that I could feel it coming out. My head was slammed against the console and a familiar voice started speaking to me in my ear.

"I told you to keep yo nose on yo face, I got somebody that want to see you."

Fear was suddenly all I knew, I remembered that being the exact thing he said before Trixie came up dead. I could feel blood from my nose seeping into my mouth. I tried to move my head but he slammed it again and told Dan,

"You ain't dead yet, drive."

Dan slowly cranked up the car unlocking the doors at the same. This was a real bad time to have some dark ass tinted windows. The car started to pull off slowly and Dan drove a few blocks up the road, holding his stomach the whole time grimacing in pain as Troy's homeboy told him which turns to make, Dan followed is directions. He must've seen the same sign as I did that said 'AMTRACK', Dan sped up knocking the nigga in the backseat backwards. He started cringing in what looked like unbearable pain but kept speeding up. The nigga in the back pounced up and hit ol boy in the head making him swerve the car a little. Dan jerked the car back and yelled,

"RUN, GO, JUMP!"

Right then I realized he was speeding up for a reason. When the nigga heard Dan yell he tried to grab my hair again except this time I wasn't gone let the nigga get away with it. I pulled my elbow up and hit that nigga dead in the mouth making him fall back a little. If I was going to die I was going to die on my own, not at the hands of some nigga I didn't even know.

Glad to see Dan was close to the curb near the grass, I took my chances not being able to think it through. Opening the door I rolled out, hitting my legs on the curb but more than half of my body was in the grass. I watched as Dan sped up some more, then I heard a gunshot and the car went out of control. I brushed myself off and tried to get up.

As I was trying to get up I noticed the blood on my knees running all the way down my legs, I felt like I was going to pass out. I had to move off the side of the road, but it was like I was stuck. my head was pounding because everything happened in a flash no one seemed to care about my bloody ass, I was obviously in need of help. I began to limp down a little flagging every car I seen, it felt like years later before a car actually pulled over and stopped. An elderly couple was nice enough to give me a lift to the train station.

They asked me if I needed to go to the hospital, but all my mouth could manage to say was no. I had no energy left to give. I just decided to fucking leave all my shit I got down here at the hotel room. I knew I wasn't going to get my money back, there was nothing I could do about that. That was the least of my worries.

Once the older couple dropped me off at the train station, I limped inside and found the nearest water fountain. Pushing the button in the fountain while bending over to its level I let the water run over my face for a second before I drank what seemed like every damn drop.

Coming back up I felt a little lightheaded. I had no time to process everything that was going on, from what the old lady said to the shit that just happened with the damn Uber driver. I bet that nigga wished he never would've signed up for the shit and it was all my fault. I so called myself looking out for him by making him not drive all the way across town in this Cali traffic. Apparently, all I did was put his life in danger. The thing that puzzled me the most was the fact that nigga got all the way to Cali so quick, made me think there was some kind of tracking device on my phone, but I was trying not to read too much into it right now. I was just going to have to have somebody check it out when I got back home, for right now my only concern was getting the fuck out of Cali.

Once I was at the front counter, the clerk told me that there wasn't a train leaving until nearly eight-forty-five and the ticket was damn near two hundred dollars just for a one-way route. On top of that, it was a two-day trip on the train. It was looking like I didn't have any other choice though. I had to do what I had to do to keep myself safe for the moment. Luckily, I had all my cash and cards on me to go ahead and pay for the ticket. I was just going to have to wait a few hours for the train to get there if it wasn't behind schedule and I prayed to God it was not.

*****

It was just now rounding towards eight-thirty and the train had actually came a little before scheduled time. Boy, I was happy than a motherfucker, them hard ass seats in the train station was hurting my ass, which didn't make the pain in my legs feel any better. I didn't even care enough to wipe the dried up blood off my pants. I was too paranoid to move and too anxious to get the fuck out of dodge. Not being able to find what I came for left me wondering what was left to tell. I'm just glad I made it out alive, that was nobody but God. As I boarded the train letting out a sigh feeling a sudden relief.

When I sat down in my seat I pulled out my phone while reaching for the leg lever to prop my feet up. The seats weren't that comfortable, and the leg rest barely came up, but the shit was going to have to do, there was no turning back now. Looking at my phone I had several missed calls and texts from Kodak, Big Boy and Tesea. I didn't know what could've come over her mind to try to call me. I figured I was going to have to be smart about every move I made from here on out. First, I decided to call Kodak back but there was no answer so, I tried texting him letting him know to call or text as soon as he could because some real shit had come up and I really needed to talk to him.

I knew Big Boy was only calling because I skipped out on work without notice, all I had to do was show up once I got there, he would never fire me, only way he could get rid of me was if I got rid of myself; I was his biggest money maker. The train pulled off as I was deep in thought, I figured it would be wise to call Tesea later, I didn't want her getting any impressions that I knew more about her than she was telling me. A part of me didn't know what to expect, not knowing if she was gone keep on playing me like the fool I apparently was for trusting in her friendship or if she was gone come clean.

CHAPTER 16

Thirty minutes into the ride, I decided to go ahead and call Tesea, I held my breath until she answered the phone. She picked up on the second ring,

"Hey girl, where the hell you been? I've been calling!" she sounded just like the friend I've always known

"Girl nowhere, something came up with my family, what's going on with you?"

"Bitch, too much, looks like I won't be getting married after all. Troy's been in the hospital beyond sick, the doctors said they don't think he'll make it," she started to cry, but it seemed so fake and nonchalant.

Not knowing what else to say I let out a deep sigh,

"Damn girl, what you mean he sick and the doctors don't think he gone make it? You think it's a mistake?"

"No, bitch he doesn't even look like himself no more, I'm just going to have to tell you all about it whenever you get home. Where did you say you was at again?"

Panic surged through my whole body, I pulled the phone away from my ear and took in a couple of deep breaths.

"Leaving my parent's house, somethings were going on with my mom. I hope Troy gets better, maybe it's a mistake girl. Try to think positive, what hospital they take him to?"

"The St. Joseph's across town, let me know when you make it girl. I really need my bestie right now, everything's going wrong right now." I rolled my eyes to the back of my head.

Shit you telling me, I thought to myself shaking my head at the same time. All I could manage to say was okay and hung up the phone. I thought I played it off pretty well. She had me wondering though, if Troy was really sick and how sick could he possibly be enough to where the doctor's didn't think he was going to make it.

Making a mental note to myself deciding I was going to find out myself by going up to the hospital. If Liah was right about Troy, then he might be willing to tell me what the hell was going on. For right now I needed to try to sit back and relax I had a long ass ride ahead of me. As soon as I closed my eyes, I remembered the good times. How me and Tesea both ended up getting each other gifts last year for Christmas, she got me two pairs of Beats Headphones one in pink and one in red. I fell in love with them the first moment I saw them, at the time I really thought she had gone all out. My gift wasn't as expensive as hers, I just thought it was the thought that counted so I got her a real gold best friend bracelet with a charm on it and I had the matching one to the set. I really thought she loved it. But now I wasn't quite sure what she liked or loved. I just wish I knew the real her, she had so many secrets. A past life I didn't know shit about, and instead of pressing her about her life story, I decided to trust her with mine. Was that a good idea? I wasn't too sure now; I wanted to believe she was the person I grew to love.

I woke up not realizing that I fell asleep, I was in a puddle of my own sweat. I couldn't remember what I was dreaming about but it had to be intense for me to wake up sweating when the train was cold as hell and I didn't have shit to cover myself up with. Checking my phone, it was dead, and the charger was left at the hotel room back in Cali.

Someone boomed over the intercom saying we were only a few hours away from the next stop;

luckily it was my stop. I just didn't know what to do when I got off, I had no way of calling a cab to take me to the airport to get my car, if it was even still there. I was praying to God that nobody fucked with it while I was gone, guess I was just going to have to wait and see, I'm sure I could find somebody that would let me use their phone at the train station.

The next few hours flew by. I just stared out the window looking at all the beautiful scenery as we passed through the cities. It turned out the person sitting next to me had a charger to fit my phone, so I was able to get a little battery juice before the train stopped at my stop. I decided to go ahead and call a cab ahead of time that way when I got there the cab would already be waiting. It seemed like that was the best idea I had in the last few weeks. Once the train came to a stop, I got up and stretched, my leg was still in pain and I noticed I still had a limp.

I walked as fast as I could to meet the cab driver. As soon as I was inside the cab, it took him no time to get me to the airport, but with the airport traffic being so bad it ended up taking us forever to actually get in the actual parking lot. And there I was thinking that my luck was starting to finally turn around. On top of that I couldn't even remember where I parked, the longer we rode around the parking lot the more money was going be coming out of my pocket. To be honest I was so tired of wasting my time and money it was ridiculous.

After a few more rounds around the parking lot, I remembered that I must've parked over by the employees cars so my car could be safe. Shit once I realized that, I already owed the motherfucking man $43.75. Taking the money out of my pockets I threw it at him, frustrated that the shit was taking longer than I thought it would. Even though not remembering where I parked my car with my fault, the way he was driving was not. I guess I shouldn't've' expected to speed around the parking lot; the man needed to make a living too. I was just impatient, nervous and paranoid all at the same time. Getting out of the cab, I limped my ass all around the parking area trying to see exactly where I had parked at. At first, I didn't see my car and I was starting to get more paranoid until I seen my baby, I almost jumped for fucking joy then I remembered my legs and decided that wasn't the best idea.

CHAPTER 17

I woke up to bright ass lights seeping through my eyelids, not remembering what the hell had happened I felt dead, I suddenly wondered if I was in heaven. That was until I heard a voice I'd been longing to hear.

"Kayla, you gone be alright ma, I'm right here I'm not going nowhere."

I could feel Kodak's hand around mine, I tried opening my eyelids slowly. Noticing that the light that I seen was the hospital lights above my head, I began to blink my eyes They came into focus and I could see Kodak's face over mine, grinning showing off them golds of his. I tried smiling but my face wouldn't move; I felt weak as fuck. I could barely speak above a whisper as I asked,

"What the hell? What am I doing here?"

I could tell by the way he was looking at me that he felt bad for me. I didn't want him to feel bad for me though, I wanted to know what the fuck was going on. How the fuck I got here, and where the fuck did he come from? The shit was hurting my head, I was trying to rack my brain to remember . so I tried to relax as best I could and wait on his explanation.

"Damn ma, them suckers must've did my shawty in for you not to have no memory, you was in a car wreck. Doctor said ya lost control of yo car and that you was already injured behind the wheel, the fuck was you thinking ma. I came up here as soon as I heard."

My memory slowly started to come back to me after he said that. I remembered breaking my car window to get my spare key, everything was still kind of a blur, but I remembered that the breaks wouldn't work and that they worked just fine before I left the car at the airport. Somebody must've been trying to kill me. From what the doctors were saying all I had was some head trauma and a broken arm. I'd better been lucky that was all I had, I just wasn't quite sure how the wreck broke my arm.

I wasn't gone feed too much into it anyway, at least Kodak was here for now, I'd better enjoy the shit while it lasted cause he just let me know that he had a show to do near South Carolina, I wouldn't be seeing his ass for weeks. Really, I didn't even know what the point was of him coming then just to tell me that bullshit. I tried to shake my head at the thought of the shit, but my head was hurting like crazy.

All I could bring myself to say to him before he was about to leave was

"Since you about to leave we might as well get a quickie in" he looked at me and laughed.

"Ma, you hurt you need to-"

I cut him off real quick, I didn't want to hear that shit, wasn't no telling when I was gone be able to see him again. Wasn't like I was in any position to be traveling like that and it wasn't like South Carolina as around the corner.

"My arm broke and my legs might hurt, but my pussy work just fine, the water still in the well."

I reached my good arm over and pulled his ass closer by his belt, sticking my hand down his pants. Leaning all awkwardly, I discovered this nigga was already hard. He grinned down at me.

"Girl, you just don't know ma."

He turned around heading towards the door, locked it and closed the blinds making sure no one could see in this time around. It made me remember the video of us fucking in my own home. He pulled down his pants and lifted up my hospital gown, kissing the bruises on my legs. He carefully separated my legs and sucked on my cl t before entering my pussy. Once again, I was in heaven, I just wanted him to stay inside of me forever. It hurt and felt so good at the same time.

It was a quickie too, Kodak's ass was done in twenty minutes. Since I couldn't get out of the bed fast enough he had to go in the bathroom to get me something to wipe myself off with, then ended up wiping me. He must've knew the struggle, I laughed to myself as he was pulling up his pants. I really didn't want him to go, I knew he had to though. Then it dawned on me that I didn't even know what hospital I was in, I guess I didn't bother to ask. After Kodak bent down and gave me a kiss I asked him,

"Black, what hospital am I at?" he was heading towards the door when he responded.

"You at St. Joseph's downtown, now get some rest, Imma call you as soon as I make it shawty."

Now my head was really pounding, from my memory of what happened before the wreck. The image of me sitting on the train with my legs propped up, waiting for it to pull off before I calle Tesea back popped in my head. I remembered when I got on the phone with her she said something about Troy being sick, about him being so sick that the doctors didn't think he was going to make it and that he was at St. Joseph's downtown. It looked like my luck was picking up, all I had to do was find him now. I waited until a nurse came back into the room, so I could make up some bullshit ass lie to get out of the room.

As soon as the nurse entered the room I told her that Troy was my brother and that I needed to let him know I was here so that he wouldn't be so worried, thinking that I'd decided to not come and see him in his time of need. The nurse looked skeptical at first, but went ahead and grabbed a wheelchair. Helping me into the wheelchair she rolled me out of the room and said I was lucky because he was only the next hallway over.

When she pulled in front of the door I told her to leave me, I made sure the nurse was gone before I rolled myself into the room using my good arm. Looking at him lying on the bed, he looked dead. Maybe Tesea wasn't lying about that. I could see his eyes open while he slowly turned his face towards me and all I wanted to do was stab him right in the eye but something told me I wouldn't have to. He was already dying, already sad and suddenly I felt bad for him; not knowing why. He opened his mouth to speak,

"Everything's not what it looks like Kay." he started to cough up a storm, he looked skinny as hell.

"I'm sorry for everything, I'm sure by now Liah told you everything, she was my heart, I never meant to hurt you. And because of my conscience this is where I am today. I can't say everything I want to because my life would be shorter, just know there's more clips, whether you believe it or not Tesea ain't who you think she is. She's evil. Man look at me, look what she's done because she thought I'd talk. She injected me with a syringe filled with a virus. Turns out it was full blown Aids. Aint no hope for me Kay. But don't worry. You don't got it."

CHAPTER 18

My mouth dropped wide open because I wasn't able to believe my ears; they had to be deceiving me. How could that shit even be possible, and what the fuck could he mean don't worry? He raped me and now he was telling me he has full-blown AIDS! Like that's just the way of life the fuck.

"How can I not worry when you talking about AIDS and shit knowing you raped me? Nobody can make you rape another motherfucker. A part of you had to want to, if not all of you."

My body was shaking with anger, I didn't know if it was because of me being so stupid or for him being a sick ass dog wanting to put all the blame on someone else. He look up towards the ceiling breathing in deeply,

"You can be mad all you like Kayla, you have every right to be, and yes you're right a part of me wanted to do it but the torture was not my idea. You have to believe me. I'm positive you haven't got all the clips yet that's just a part of her game. You're not going to catch her at her own game Kayla, she's been doing this shit for years."

He started shaking his head and I could see tears rolling down his face, he didn't even look the same no more. Not being able to find the words to say, I just sat back in the wheelchair trying to wrap my mind around everything. Basically, according to Troy, shit was far from over and I was stuck playing this bitch's game. There was just one thing I had left to ask,

"What really happened to your parents Troy?"

He looked back in my direction and wiped his face off with his left hand,

"I'm dying anyway right? What's wrong with me shedding a little light on the past?" he sounded like he was more so trying to convince his self I could tell there was fear in his voice; something horrible had happened.

"Regina and Paul took me into their home when I was very young, too young to know what was going on around me. They always loved and cared for me like I was their own, they couldn't have any more children and Tesea was technically their only child. They wanted a little boy, but they still treated Tesea like a princess.

There was just something about her that had always rubbed me the wrong way. She never texted me when I was younger, barely even notice me, if anything she looked at me in disgust shaking her head at the same time. Then beauty hit for the both of us and I would always catch her hiding in the closet touching herself to playboy magazines that so happened to be Paul's. Nevertheless, her obsession with sex grew more and more every day.

She started touching me in my sleep, sometimes I'd wake up to her kissing my dick and me not knowing any better I let her. She would watch Regina and Paul having sex through the crack of their bedroom door touching herself moaning all at the same time. One day I was walking by as she was looking through the crack of the door and I noticed Paul looking back at her. It seemed like it just made him go harder, like he knew she was watching the whole time.

Eventually she started making moves on him and he'd spank her and call her a nasty ass little girl but by then she was 15. Seeing that the shit she was doing didn't work, over the years she'd started taking Regina's sleeping pills, handfuls of them and would crush them up and put them in his food, drinks, or anything he would consume instantly knocking him out. She would take knives and slickly cut the hairs from around his balls. That's when Regina caught her and didn't know what to do because Tesea had that a knife in her hands. I think that's when she became afraid of her, not knowing what to do with her because she loved her daughter, the only child she had been able to have. Teaea started getting creative after she found out how to drug Paul, she'd tie him up and suck him up right at the dining room table with the windows wide open. Then would get a strap-on and shove it right in Paul's mouth. Once Paul started to refuse to eat anything from the house, Tesea started getting furious.

She threatened me, saying that she'd kill me too if I didn't help her come up with something. She didn't want Paul to live anymore because of the simple fact he found out that somehow, he was being drugged and kept waking up feeling violated. Fast forwarding a little bit, I called our grandparents off a pay phone and told them that we'd be coming to stay for a while and if anybody asked we were with them.

So, the alibi was set, I waited for Tesea outside in the dark while she brutally stabbed Paul over and over again and set the house on fire, she killed Regina too because she figured she had no more use for her. Bad thing about it was she did a shitty job and almost got caught up. That's why she needed me because the old lady, that always live next door, called the cops right away and they were able to identify the bodies. We had an alibi, so we were ruled out instantly.

Tesea wasn't satisfied enough with that and decided we needed to move and change our last names and that's what we did. Once we moved here Tesea begin to act like a normal person again until she met you, then the game started all over again. You were never more to her, rather somebody she just wanted to be or somebody to make as miserable as herself. She had let me live my life as I chose when we first got here. She just told me I could never go back to Liah, and Liah could never come down here. If she would've never met, you she would have never started acting fucking crazy again. Holding shit over my head like I was the one that killed Paul and Regina. But she was sure going to make it look like that, if I didn't play by her rules I'd be in jail for life. Things started going left when Trixie started finding out more about who Tesea really was and who I was. Once Teasea got wind of Trixie speaking to Liah it was all over from there. She thought that eventually I started running my mouth just to be with Liah. Shit, she took care of that real quick. I knew I told her too much, but I figured she'd be safe thousands of miles away, and just in case you were wondering the men at my bachelor party were not my homeboys; it was all a setup from the start. She set it up to make everything in your life fall apart so she could take your place. When I found out Liah was dead I confronted her, but from the looks of it she planned it out from the start and stuck a syringe in my neck filled with tainted blood contaminated with AIDS." I shook my head and couldn't find the words to say, so I had the nurse come take me to my room and I passed out. I woke up with tears in my eyes and once I looked at my hands to wipe them away I saw Chris. I was about to ask why the hell he was here until I saw Teasea's head bobbing up and down on his dick. I fainted right back to sleep.

Chapter 29

My breathing was so unsteady, I was going into a panic attack; I just knew it. The doctor's rushed in to check my vital signs to see how I was doing then they escorted everybody out of the room, I could hear them in the distance. Everything seemed so far away, but yet so close. The nurse was right beside me and I could hear her telling me that everything was going to be ok, I was just having an anxiety attack which was quite normal under the circumstances. I wanted to believe her ass so bad, but inside I felt like I was dying, feeling like I done took all I could take.

All the while I was hoping that my eyes had deceived me. Where the fuck had Chris come from? And why the hell would he still choose to disrespect me in my face? Sleep or not sleep, I was the one in the hospital going through it. My eyes slowly came into focus, and my breathing had slowed down a little. Most of the nurses and doctors left the room when everything became under control.

Tear's began to pour out rolling down my cheeks, burning my eyes and what was fucked up, I couldn't even use both hands to cover my face. I didn't want nobody to see me like this, and for the most part, I didn't even know why I was crying.

It was just too much, I used my good hand to wipe the tears away and just laid back and started humming to myself hoping I would just fall asleep to my own rhythm. It wasn't a big surprise when I wasn't able to. Furthermore, once the last nurse left, in came Chris with Tesea a couple steps behind him. I didn't have the energy to roll my eyes the way I wanted to, they barely rolled at all but I was sure they caught my damn drift. Tesea's bitch ass rushed to my side like she was so damn concerned, and that's when the first time throughout our friendship I saw this bitch for who she truly was; a trifling ass hoe.

I was utterly disgusted at the sight of her, then I remembered what Troy said about the game she was playing. I couldn't believe that it took me this long to realize that my best friend wasn't really my friend, probably never was. Until I was able to heal completely I would have to play this bitch game, before she decided for it to be game over and I was dead too. So, for right now I was going to have to shoot the shit. Looking at this bitch just made me want to go in on her ass, instead I mustered up a half smile.

"Where the hell did you come from?"

The both of them looked at one another.

"Kodak told me what was going on shawty."

Chris looked me over making me just want to cut his damn dick off. Disgusting ass bastard.

"For one, I ain't your damn shawty. So, it isn't any of your concern, I ain't dead, you didn't have to come check on me." he stood there looking stupid like he was at a loss for words. *Good*, I thought to myself, *ain't shit for the nigga to say.*

"Girl, you know once I heard what was going on I was going to be here to support you, it's just crazy that you and Troy in the same hospital, that's really how I found out boo, I'm so sorry this happened to you."

Blinking my eyes I continued to look dead at her, without saying anything. She continued,

"I wish it was me instead of you, you already know I would take your place in a heartbeat. It just kills me to see you in here like this."

I almost choked and tried to fight the urge to go off on her crazy ass; this bitch really had nerve. Boy, she was playing the shit out of the role. No wonder it took my ass so long to believe the shit. This bitch wanted to be me and now I could see it plain as day. This motherfucker wanted to ruin my life, wanted to prove that she was better at being me than I was. I had to keep reminding myself to hold it together because wasn't shit I could do right now but get myself killed.

I thought to myself if this was the bitch Chris was talking about all along. The friend he fucked with but didn't want to tell me who she was. Shit, I knew it had to be her now which made me wonder why the fuck he couldn't've just came out and told me straight up instead of letting me find out the hard way. Although, when a nigga tell you watch your friends 10 times out of 10, the nigga know something and you need to start looking at bitches sideways.

Me being me, just never believing anybody close to me could do me so dirty. It's like nobody knew the real me behind the pole, like I was living a secret life, but shit, aren't we all. Lately, I've been feeling like my life was a movie or a book, because those are the only places you see so many fucked up things happen in a short amount of time. But in all those movies starred a dingy ass white girl making dumb decisions; I guess that made me the star with the exception of being dingy and white. I was the naïve motherfucker that everybody was getting down on. Looking at Teasea I wondered why she didn't want to be herself, she was a beautiful girl, but like the old Lady said, "she got evil all over her", which made her ugly as could be..

"Thanks for coming girl, I'm glad you're here. Even with all the things going on with Troy, I know you're devastated, you really shouldn't be worried about me, you should be there for your sibling, I mean husband to be."

I couldn't help myself, the shit just flew out my mouth and it was too late to take it back. Now why the fuck did I have to say that shit, hopefully she didn't catch it.

■■

I could see Chris looking uncomfortable as fuck and I still couldn't figure out why he was really here. If he really had talked to Kodak and found out from him, then why didn't he come with him. Or why would he come anyway if he knew I wasn't knocked off instead of just sending a simple as text, there would've been no love lost, I was over his ass.

That didn't mean that I wanted to see Tesea's ass sucking him up though, that shit was really just beyond disrespectful to go behind your own best friend like that, especially while she was laying in the hospital bed right behind you, come on bitch, she knew I wasn't in no damn coma. All this shit was going through my head while Tesea was on the side of me trying to play it cool, I see right through her ass though, she was thirty-eight hot.

"What sibling girl, you know I ain't got no family like that anymore, besides my grandparents and they all the way on the west coast, I was thinking bitch I should go ahead and marry Troy so that we know it's real. That it was always real as I want him to know I'm always here for him come even in my worst of situations such as this, it would be a miracle if he was able to pull through, matter of fact I'm going to check on him, call me when they discharge you love." she snapped her head so hard that I thought her neck broke, she was gone in a heartbeat without giving me a chance to say another word.

Chris was still standing there looking at me like a damn fool, he looked over his shoulder, I guess to see if Tesea was gone, which made me wonder what the fuck he was so scared of.

"The doctor said you can leave in the next couple of hours, they said it was wise if you didn't lift anything or try to lift yourself and that it should be 6 weeks or longer before your arm heals."

I could feel it in my bones that there was more he had to say, but was hesitant to say it, so I just smiled and waited to be let go.

"We gotta get out of here, like now! I'll explain in the car." Given the circumstances I didn't question it.

Chris helped me out of the bed and carried me bridal style, we took the fire escape stairs out of the hospital and got in his car when we reached the parking lot. He burned rubber trying to get out of the lot, headed to my house.

Chris pulled in the driveway and rushed to get out to grab the wheelchair off the back seat. I wasn't sure why I needed one, but I was told it was best to stay off my feet as little as possible. The hospital didn't give us the wheelchair, this nigga already had one, which got my brain thinking all sorts of shit; like this nigga knew what was going to happen the whole time. Once Chris was inside, he closed the door behind me and began walking room to room checking windows and behind TVs and everything he could look behind.

" Well, what the hell are you looking for and tell me what the fuck you was really doing at the hospital besides getting your dick sucked?" he stopped looking for whatever in turned towards me

"You really that damn dumb? Come on now, do I really have to tell you what the fuck I'm looking for. Open your eyes to the shit has been going on around you man. She's been bugging your house., setting up cameras. Having mother fuckers follow you around, all types of shit. I told you a long time ago you got to watch who you are around. The bitch is evil and I'm in too deep to walk away or she'll have my ass arrested for a job I did for her a long as time ago the bitch paid me well though."

He paused before continuing,

"Now I'm going to go that way I won't end up like Troy. I can promise you that coma shit is exactly what it's supposed to look like but if you go back to the hospital his life will end sooner than it was supposed to. The Bitch is evil, I don't know how many times I got to say it. She had me come to the hospital just so you could see her suck on my dick Kayla, it's all a part of her plan. So for right now, try to keep your distance and keep an eye out for Kodak. She want everything you done ever had or ever wanted. She been a mark from the get go. Shit, I almost forgot to show you this, take a real quick look, then I'm going to bounce."

He pulled out his phone and showed me a clip that I was never supposed to see, the clip showed Tesea's charm on the bracelet I got for her on Christmas dangling in front of the camera when Troy was raping me.

Chris ran out the door after showing me, the shit wasn't even worth my tears anymore; I finally knew the truth. Common sense told me there was more to find out; I had a strong feeling that Kodak used to fuck with her way before me. She was the girl he had been talking about, I picked up my phone and called him repeatedly leaving message after message, hours later, he still hadn't responded.

I started to get worried, but I told myself to relax. So, I turned on the news and there he was, they were saying he was arrested for rape after one of his shows. They showed a half image of the girl and there she was; Tesea. I threw my phone causing it to knock over an open water bottle and the pieces separated as it hit the floor. When I picked up my battery I noticed a very small black circle thing that I'd never seen before, there was a little red light on it and it look like a small microphone.

Holding my breath, I very carefully removed whatever it was and threw it in a little pool of water from the bottle on the floor and stepped on it. Thinking back on it, that might have been what Chris was looking for which had me wondering what the hell Teasea really had really had to make him do some of her dirty work. I would have to find out some other time because that was the least of my worries.

Placing my battery back in my phone, I set it on the counter and went looking for my Macbook so I could find out when visitation was up there where they were holding Kodak. With only a few clicks on their website, I found out it was on Saturdays, so I booked a flight to Columbia, South Carolina, and decided to go to the clinic to get a STD test immediately after,

How the fuck could I just go off Troy's word? For all I knew he could've injected my ass with the bullshit too! It would only take a week or so to find out after I took the test, by that time I'd be in South Carolina, not thinking twice I called a cab and headed out to the clinic. I had to wait almost 2 hours before being seen.

After it was all over, I had the cab driver take me straight to the airport I was ready to be down for Kodak the way he wanted me to be. I waited hours before boarding the plane, it would take less than 7 hours to make it. I slept the whole way there with nothing but Tesea in my head.

It was almost time for my visit with Kodak. I had spoke to him briefly, long enough for him to put me down on the list. I was grateful as hell that he remembered my number. Otherwise, I would not have been able to see him at all and it would have been a dry ass waste of money and a trip. Thirty minutes later I was sitting behind a big glass window witness. See my baby. It was cold as hell in there.

The seats were metal and there was only a black phone on the side of the booth, I waited for was seem like forever before I actually saw him.

As Kodak was coming out, his hands were getting unshackled. He looked like somebody had hit him in the face with a rock. He looked so tired, restless for a man with so much money; he looked helpless.

Kodak sat down, the guard left and closed the door behind him before I picked up the black phone, I noticed that my phone had vibrated. I knew that I wasn't supposed to have it inside the visitation area so I took a quick glance at the email, not being able to believe my eyes.

I quickly put my phone away and picked up the black phone, which Kodak had in his hands already on the other side of the glass. His ass did not look pleased. *that's what my ass get for not being as slick as I thought I was*, I looked at him stunned through the glass.

"Just tell me what happened, you look bad Black, and I wasn't stunting my phone like that. I was checking out something important, that's besides the point, talk nigga." I can tell he was hesitating a little before he spoke.

"Look, I just know I never knew this bitch was your friend first and foremost, to me her name was always Tesea and she looked a lot different back then. Remember the night I was at a house and my phone went off? That was her, and she was also the girl I was talking about when I took you around the city in all honesty. I haven't seen her since I broke it off. I would've never known that was her that night at the club with you. At the club she never said nothing to me in person, but she would always blow my phone off the rip. The shit that's going on now ain't nothing but lies, the bitch rotten! I ain't even worried about it, God got me believe that just hold it down for a nigga if you really feeling me ma."

I stared at him for a minute, not sure how I should tell him this, taking in a deep breath. I finally worked up enough courage to tell him.

"Black, before you start saying anything else listen to me. I'm not going anywhere and the best reason I could think of is because I'm pregnant."

To be continued.....

Manufactured by Amazon.ca
Bolton, ON